ABSOLUTE AWAY

ALSO BY LANCE OLSEN

ABSOLUTE AWAY

— a novel —

LANCE OLSEN

DZANC
BOOKS

**DZANC
BOOKS**

2580 Craig Rd.
Ann Arbor, MI 48103
www.dzancbooks.org

Library of Congress Cataloguing-in-Publication Data Available Upon Request

First Edition: April 2024
Cover design by Matthew Revert
Interior design by Michelle Dotter

ISBN 9781950539956

Printed in the United States of America

10   9   8   7   6   5   4   3   2   1

for Andi,
all time this time always

I

Different moments in time hang in space like sheets. The world is made up of these frozen moments, great meta-images, and we just hop from one to the next.... And the same might apply to space. Nothing is truly anchored on any day, nor in any place.

—Olga Tokarczuk

THIS NIGHT, THIS MAY

Months shy of three, woozy from sleep, Edie Metzger experiences the night of the burning not as a neat succession of events, but rather as bright flashes flying at her.

EDIE IN AMBER

Far inside her dream, where everything lasts a thousand years, she hears her parents' low voices floating up the hallway, then all at once close by, suffusing her room, lulling her heart, lamp light pouring in around their silhouettes as if love were a haze that clings to the skin, feels her father's enormous hands lift her bundled in a flannel nightie (her favorite: freckled with rosebuds, ruffled along the hem) from her pink blanket, her crib, draping Edie over his shoulder, forearm supporting her rump, palm to the back of her skull, feels her mother's lips brush her forehead, and Edie is floating, footsteps clumping beneath her, cozy, content, carried inside her parents' conversation as she floats in her father's arms down the floating staircase and out into frigid air, where her world transfigures into a clanking U-Bahn carriage tearing through black, and then this floating again, now through a havoc of noisy bodies and faces deformed by the weird shimmerings throughout Berlin's Opernplatz—a name, a place, Edie won't learn this evening or any other.

WRITTEN ON AIR

Traveling in her father's arms has always meant elation for Edie, a tram or bus ride an atlas of benevolent surprises. Traveling in his arms means anything is possible, which means maybe this evening her parents and she will cross the gauzy borders separating humans from fairytales, step inside a hut made of Christmas cookies and raspberry icing where Edie's porcelain doll Eva with real blonde hair has invited them to tea, in the garden of which bunnies and nymphs play dominos made from shortbread on the banks of a brook flowing with liquid moonlight.

THE LAW OF TRULY LARGE HOPE

Or this:

So-called impossible events are sometimes referred to as miracles. This would be incorrect in any strict sense. It is more accurate to say that with a large enough sample size any outrageous thing you can imagine is likely to happen occasionally.

Think of it this way:

An unfathomable number of events occur every second on earth. That means extremely unlikely ones must occur nearly every second. Events called impossible aren't therefore impossible. They occur regularly, the result of probabilities.

John Edensor Littlewood, British mathematician, proposed in 1986 what has come to be known as Littlewood's Law: that we should expect, statistically speaking, one-in-a-million incidents to happen to us at a rate of about one per month.

In this sense we can consider miracles relatively commonplace.

AN UNBURNED ROSE

Long live my heart, the machine of my thinking, the essayist Ander Monson will write thirty-four years later.

A COMMOTION OF RED BALLOONS

It never occurred to Edie to question why her mother and father woke her long after she had fallen asleep, after her dinner and her bath and her bedtime story and her last kiss of the day, why they hoisted her out of her dream (in which she was snuggling on the cool living room parquet floor with the family's white cat, Schaum, nothing transpiring except the wondrous softness of his fur, the steady pulse of his purr), because for Edie all time is this time, and maybe tonight they will sit around the table in her doll Eva's hut and sip tea amid a commotion of red balloons, speaking of large lollipops and pumpkins like princes and princesses do.

BLUEPRINT OF THE ORDINARY WORLD

Which means maybe to reach the hut, her parents and Edie will get to sleep on a train and make new friends with fellow passengers, one of whom will be a polite zebra or slightly haughty giraffe wearing a monocle. Edie would miss her cousins back in the city, but she could soon crayon pretty picture-letters to them requesting the honor of their presence at her endless party—even if eventually, given the daunting abundance of them, she would be required to find a considerably larger hut, perhaps one inside a gigantic hollowed-out candy cane with a door constructed from daffodils and windows from her favorite lullabies.

THE IMPERFECT AS PARADISE

When, she wonders, will my next birthday reach me?

A LIST OF INSUFFICIENT KNOWLEDGE ON A COLD NIGHT

Only what happens is this: Edie's mother and father pushing their
way through a havoc of bodies and faces gathered in the long wide
square on the far side of Unter den Linden between the Opera House
and Humboldt University, at the end of which hulks St. Hedwig's
Cathedral.

Edie doesn't know the names of these buildings.

She has no idea where she is other than in her father's arms, he
every once in a while repositioning her weight from right shoulder
to left, left to right, because of the difficulty inherent in keeping such
massive love airborne.

EARTH TENDENCIES

Edie doesn't understand she is inhabiting a moment called the middle
of May within a number called 1933.

THE SEA YOU CAN'T SEE

Sixty-two years later, John Berger will write in a novel entitled *To the
Wedding*, which has nothing to do with the evening Edie Metzger
is living: *The waters change all the while and stay the same only on the
map.*

DISTRIBUTION OF AMAZEMENT

What Edie understands is how people are jostling her father and her, how floating has become lurching, coziness vague unease, how perspective has gone askew, the square tilted, structures canted, and there is a scrawny man in uniform shouting behind a podium because why?

STUDY IN MAGIC

Two hundred and sixty-three years before Edie asks herself that question, this: while staging the Nativity, the choirmaster at the Cologne Cathedral (his name lamentably lost) three hundred sixty miles to Berlin's west became irate at how loud and fidgety the children watching the performances had become, and so he set about devising a remedy.

He hurried over to the local candymaker, a man about whom history has forgotten everything except the mauve mole on his forehead, and asked the fellow to create sugar sticks he might use as a form of distraction-as-attention.

But not just any sugar sticks.

The choirmaster requested they be crooked into staffs reminiscent of those used by the shepherds who visited the infant Jesus, colored white for Christ's purity, and laced with crimson to represent Our Savior's spilled blood.

Even though the children might mistakenly believe they were enjoying themselves, they would in fact be learning an important lesson about virtue, pain, and piety, the little snot-nosed brats.

ALL THOSE PRETTY FLAMES

Edie watches all those pretty flames rising from the pyres, smoke making her eyes sting like when her mother grills bratwursts in a skillet, which means those men over there are grilling books, which means everyone will get to sample some soon, and she can't wait to discover what fairytales taste like.

ELEVATION AS OPTIMISM : 1

Edie's father sets her down among an understory of legs and she immediately attempts scrabbling up again.

WORDS AS WEATHER

Edie can't understand any of the words the scrawny man is busy unleashing into the night, but she can sense them moving through her body like a storm.

EDIE METZGER'S MARVELOUSNESS ACKNOWLEDGED

She relishes the radiant heat on her face, the outbursts of sparks, the reflections of the bonfires in the windows of the buildings surrounding her. Ashes wafting down remind her of the light snow that wafted down during her first visit to a winter market over the holidays (the candied almonds, the carved nutcrackers, the soft gingerbread, the endless rows of stalls, the endless strings of lights), a visit that might have occurred last week, or last year, yet that Edie is convinced was held throughout the land to commemorate her marvelousness.

THE COCKROACH GAME

Listen: some children are born It. There is no way around this fact. These children are called The Roach. The Roach stuffs Its ears with cotton and sits at a table across from three other children. One shuffles a deck of cards and deals five to each player, including The Roach, explaining the rules, which, because of the cotton in Its ears, The Roach cannot hear. Thus the game commences. The other children's faces sometimes turn serious, sometimes unlock into laughter. Sometimes the children cover their eyes with their palms and sometimes raise their hands to their throats and pantomime choking. The Roach tries to discern a pattern, glean the laws that guide this country, and adjust Its moves accordingly, always to no end. When It asks a question, the others go about their business as if no one has spoken. A suspicion grows within It that the rules may change now and then for no discernable reason. This might account for the eruptions of horror and delight on the other children's countenances. The game must be played every day. From time to time one of the children who is not The Roach stands and leaves the table, only to be replaced by another. Over the years, they grow up. Over the decades, they grow old. One by one they die while playing. Eyelids half shut, eyes beclouding with light fungus, they remain upright at their posts. In the end only The Roach is left (although It is aware It has won nothing) and must, It knows, now hang Itself to bring the game to graceful conclusion. This can take quite some time.

ELEVATION AS OPTIMISM : 2

Her father sets Edie down among the forest of legs again and again she attempts scrabbling toward yes.

FIRE FROM HEAVEN AS ANVIL LIGHTNING

A miracle is an event described by those to whom it was told by people who did not see it, the American anarchist Elbert Hubbard submitted in 1909, while in 1976 the British evolutionary biologist Richard Dawkins pointed out that a belief in them would amount to some bizarre and useless subversion of Occam's Razor.

GLOBAL POSITIONING : 1

If that is true, however, Edie wonders, back on her father's right shoulder, where is Santa Claus?

THESE SMELLS

Gasoline fumes.

Particulate haze.

The oniony reek of human dampness.

THESE SOUNDS

University students, their professors, the rectors, curious bystanders, many carrying torches: laughing, chanting, clapping each other on the back in recognition and good cheer.

GLOBAL POSITIONING : 2

And her presents?

DERIVATION OF BUTCHERS

Edie doesn't know Moses's parting of the Red Sea probably had less to do with amazement than with the shallow water covering an underlying reef exposed during strong winds, nor that her given name derives from a combination of two Old English words—*ead*, meaning *wealth* or *fortune*, and *gyð*, meaning *war*, nor that her surname, *Metzger*, is a South German/Ashkenazi occupational one meaning *butcher*, a business the family has worked in for six generations despite a swarm of financial difficulties feeding off them like a school of remora.

WHAT READING FEELS LIKE

Edie may be elated by what she sees. She may be frightened. She can't make up her mind. She studies her father's face for clues, comes up empty-handed.

MAN IN THE BROWN MACINTOSH

An indistinct drizzle commences. The drizzle turns to rain. The rain intensifies. The gatherers remain undeterred. Some break into song, some into the eerie incantations that have been passed through the crowd on sheets of paper.

Next to Edie stands a heavyset man in his thirties, hands in the pockets of his brown macintosh, eyebrows thick as furry caterpillars.

Edie wants to make them her pets.

The man cries without sound as he observes the growing fires, his face becoming older by the minute, as if he has already lived fifty lifetimes and just received news that he must live an infinite number more.

Edie notices her father noticing.

He turns and says to the weeping man: Excuse me. I don't mean to— Are you—?

The man in the brown macintosh shrugs.

Without taking his eyes off the conflagration, he replies: How can anyone possibly have thought you could have made a sane realm out of these people?

LOGIC OF NIGHTFALL

If it becomes dark outside when Daddy lights the candles on our Christmas tree, Edie considers, then where is our Christmas tree now?

She raises her head off her father's shoulder, surveying.

SHIP OF THESEUS

Edie takes for granted her parents have never been apart.

There was never a period they didn't know each other, love each other, weren't her mother and father. They are two halves of the same devoted creature whose goal in life is to exalt their exquisite princess.

What else could plausibly be the case?

HISTORY AS FORCEPS : 1

When the rumors started circulating through their apartment block, Edie's parents agreed they had to go see with their own eyes.

Granted: all this nonsense would soon be over, this barbarism, this mean clarity, and life return to the un-strange. It was only a matter of time before those idiots in power were thrown out on their ears, before rational minds would again prevail. How could it be otherwise?

Still, they had to witness the lunacy themselves.

They had to show their daughter the calamity called their country.

We still live in a democracy, Edie's mother said.

At the end of the day, Edie's father said, the police and military are on *our* side.

Tomorrow, they tried to convince themselves, would see the evolution of a new syntax. This place, barely sixty years old, scarcely recovered from an unrelenting war and its aftermath, is merely struggling through some growing pains. Once upon a time, the same was true in France, America.

Just like people, no country becomes self-aware without grief.

For despots, knowledge is always a risk, Edie's father told Edie's mother this morning over breakfast before heading off to debone meat, trim, tie, grind, tenderize, weigh, wrap in newspaper, price, feign courtesy and interest in others. They want to reduce intelligence to cinders and soot. We will be watching. We will remember.

Some of us will be watching, Edie's mother said, pouring coffee for them. Some of us will be carrying the books for them.

Fewer than you think.

More than you hope.

Good people outnumber bad in the world, Edie's father said, testing the phrase on his tongue to see if it held any taste of truth.

You believe that?

What else is there to believe?

Lots of things, Edie's mother answered. She runneled cream cheese across a bagel for her husband, then one for herself. There are lots of other things you can believe.

Name one.

That there is no reason things should be easy to understand.

Edie's father turned this over, said: Name another.

That people are neither good nor bad. That they are merely themselves. And if enough of them start doing something, no matter how stupid, no matter where or when, others will start imitating them. It's exactly like monkeys, only with more developed vocal cords.

FABIAN : THE STORY OF A MORALIST

The man in the macintosh's name is Erich Kästner. Edie doesn't know he is the only author to show up tonight to see his own books dispersed into smoke. He will remain here, weeping, until someone recognizes him and calls out his name, at which point he will vanish into the fuss.

Erich's most well-known novel, *Emil and the Detectives*, will be spared.

All his others, including *Fabian: The Story of a Moralist*, will be torn up and chucked into the communal amnesia.

While *Emil and the Detectives* is a children's book reflecting Erich's belief in the regenerative powers of youth, unusual only in its un-generic gritty realism, *Fabian: The Story of a Moralist* is anything but.

According to the authorities, it is a novel that strays too far with its description of Berlin as a madhouse rife with beggars and brothels, filth and vacuous sex, lesbian debauchery and elegant male actors seduced by stunning boys, unfaithful spouses and a plenitude of suicide. It refers to Humboldt University as *an institution for moronic children*, to the city's cathedral as *the main fire station*, and boasts short, acerbic passages like this: *When an older man walked into the room for the purpose of enjoying himself, he found what he had expected, a naked, sixteen-year-old girl. Unfortunately, she was his daughter.*

Nearly as bad, *Fabian* exploits techniques from degenerate

modernist film, such as rapid cuts and montages, to better capture the frenetic whirl of the Weimar Republic's undoing, which is to say it incarnates corruption in its very form.

There must be limits.

It's either hierarchy or it's anarchy, the authorities said.

Despite what Erich observes done to his work tonight, his fervent opposition to the regime, his repeated interrogations by the Gestapo over the next few years, and his expulsion from the national writers' guild for *the culturally Bolshevist attitude in his writings*, he will choose to remain in Germany, unlike many other intellectuals, scientists, and artists, live in his broken home a broken man, an alcoholic passing his nights in bars and bordellos, his days producing inoffensive apolitical writing on the grounds that after the war he will chronicle Germany's ruin from the inside out.

He will do so for another reason as well: to be closer to his bedridden mother in Dresden, to whom he will pen a loving postcard every day.

Decades later, Erich will win the Hans Christian Andersen Medal for his lasting contribution to children's literature, be nominated four times for the Nobel Prize, and have many streets (not to mention an asteroid) named after him.

Although never substantiated, rumors will circulate to this day that Erich's biological father was the family's Jewish doctor, Emil Zimmermann.

All that, however, lies in his future.

Right now Erich Kästner is a heavyset man with furry eyebrows, hunkering against the steady rain among the nearly seventy thousand gathered in and around Opernplatz, weeping quietly as the best parts of him are converted into heterogeneous particulates.

VOICE AT THE END OF THE MIND

Edie forgets for a minute whether she is asleep or awake, rests her cheek on her father's shoulder, closes her eyes, and the scrawny man's bad-weather voice rumbling through her body becomes her first sweet bite of gingerbread amid snowflakes sifting down in the winter market becomes a haughty monocled giraffe sitting across from her on the train becomes a barrel-chested man with shiny face and shiny hair and rows of shiny coins pinned to his chest stooping slightly to pay Edie Metzger homage.

I AM WHAT IS AROUND ME

What beautiful blue Aryan eyes your little girl has, the barrel-chested man tells her parents.

A GARDEN FULL OF FLOWERS

Twenty-five years before that man speaks that sentence, another, Hermann Minkowski, professor of mathematics at the Federal Institute of Technology in Zurich, endured what he believed to be one of the laziest, least interested or interesting students he had ever had the misfortune to teach.

The idler's name was Albert Einstein.

Einstein skipped most lectures and, when he did now and again deign to turn up, slumped in his seat, arms crossed, taking no notes, acutely unpassionate about what he later referred to as the gunmetal monotone of mathematics.

Yet Minkowski never stopped following (with increasing regard and respect) the reception of his former student's ideas as they surfaced—

especially those revolving around the special theory of relativity put forward in 1905.

It was the sort of theory, Minkowski understood very well, that would soon have been put forward by someone else had Einstein been only a bit slower. But he was lucky enough to be at the right place at the right thought, connect the dots faintly faster than other physicists sprinting beside him in the same cerebral natatorium.

Still, Einstein's ideas didn't make much impact until September 21, 1908, when Minkowski delivered a lecture entitled "Space and Time" at the eightieth Assembly of German Natural Scientists and Physicians in Cologne. His aim, in part, was to draw attention to what his former student had accomplished by representing Einstein's algebraic equations in terms of geometry through what has come to be known as the Minkowski Diagram—and that made all the difference.

Less than a year later, Minkowski (gold pince-nez; handlebar mustache; tight abbreviated mouth) was walking to class after a heavy lunch, packed in various prickly layers of wool against January's blue bluster, when he noticed an ache near his navel.

A busy day spread out before him, so he decided to pay the ache no heed.

By the time he had finished speaking, however, a low-grade nausea had fastened onto that ache, and by the time his wife called him down to dinner several hours after that in their overstated house, the professor had become aware of a certain puffiness in his lower abdomen, which he chalked up to an annoying case of gas.

In the middle of the night his bloated appendix burst.

By noon the next day Minkowski was dead.

At forty-four years old.

In his obituary for the professor, David Hilbert, mathematician at the University of Göttingen, wrote: *Since my student years Minkowski was my best, most dependable friend who supported me with all the depth and loyalty that was so characteristic of him. Our science, which we loved above all else, brought us together.*

It seemed to us a garden full of flowers.

Einstein remained mute regarding his mentor's passing.

HYPERSURFACE OF THE PRESENT

Edie opens her eyes, assuming they are still closed. Her point of view is packed with a lady's lush fur coat hovering fewer than seven centimeters from her nose. Reflexively, Edie reaches out to stroke it just above the shocked recipient's left breast, intuiting why the lady seems so happy (clown face pancaked white, distended lips red as Christmas): being devoured alive by such a fluffy bear at a snail's pace must be the very definition of glorious.

AFTER THE FINAL YES

Edith, her mother says, tugging the back of her flannel nightie, *no.*

SECRET LIFE OF WARDROBES

Which as luck would have it leads to a realization in the heart of Edie's heart: when these people jammed around her leave this square—that clown-faced lady, the pointy beard followed by the squat man, the old woman defeated by obesity beside him—they will cease to exist.

How could they exist if not part of Edie's knowledge?

No: those people will return to their homes, step up into their wardrobes, close the doors behind them, raise their arms to their sides, and turn into human T's, just like that nice man Jesus did on the cross, only with better posture.

FELIS CATUS

Cats, needless to say, will constitute the sole exception. They will continue going about their business even when Edie isn't there to revel in them, because cats are cats and hence perfect in every way and essential to the flawless unfolding of the cosmos.

THE DEAD MAKE A NOISE LIKE WINGS

Why is everybody waving at the sky, Daddy? Edie whispers into her father's ear through her grogginess, lifting her right arm to join them.

HISTORY AS FORCEPS : 2

Several weeks earlier, students in thirty-four university cities across Germany met with their professors and Nazi party officials to discuss which publications needed to leave the planet forever.

Four days ago, the students in Berlin raided the libraries of the Institute of Sexual Research, founded in 1919 across the way in the Tiergarten by the Jewish homosexual physician Magnus Hirschfeld (who by chance was out of the country), dragged most of its contents into the square, and started constructing the pyres, often with the help of the police.

We will not compromise with communists, Jews, sexual deviants, and corrupting foreign influences, the students averred. *We want to hold the books high before throwing them into the fire so that we can celebrate the beginning of the conclusive eradication of depravity.*

More and more books from other libraries in the area were added, about twenty thousand in all, among them ones by:

Isaac Babel

Walter Benjamin

Ernst Bloch

Bertolt Brecht

Joseph Conrad

John Dos Passos

Fyodor Dostoyevsky

Theodore Dreiser

Friedrich Engels

F. Scott Fitzgerald

Sigmund Freud

André Gide

Ernest Hemingway

Hermann Hesse

Victor Hugo

Aldous Huxley

James Joyce

Helen Keller

D. H. Lawrence

Georg Lukács

Rosa Luxemburg

Thomas and Heinrich Mann

Robert Musil

Vladimir Nabokov

Erich Maria Remarque

Upton Sinclair

Leo Tolstoy

Leon Trotsky

Oscar Wilde

and Arnold Zweig.

The Student Association invited Propaganda Minister Joseph Goebbels to speak at the festivities, which he gladly did, surrounded by members of the Nazi Students' League, brownshirts, SS, Hitler Youth groups, and curious onlookers.

Goebbels wanted to hold the burning late at night rather than in broad daylight for two reasons. First, he appreciated the fact that bonfires would create in his audience a subliminal connection to their great Nordic past, conjure mythic, primal images connoting the pure German mind cleansing the decadence rampant throughout the nation. Second, he understood holding such a spectacle after midnight would induce a wavery state of consciousness in the spectators, an ecstatic unreality part Walpurgisnacht, part spiritual ritual, and part patriotic folk festival.

In the distance, a brass band played.

THE AMEN PROTOCOL

In a study conducted by the University of Connecticut and Georgetown University, fifty-seven percent of adults surveyed said they believed that god's intervention could save a family member, even when physicians have assured them that any further treatment would be futile. For the terminal praying for miracles, the clinicians at Johns Hopkins Cancer Center developed the Affirm, Meet, Educate, No Matter What script designed to help negotiate the fact that no miracle will be forthcoming while never stating the obvious and continuing to keep patient trust intact as the incurable slowly but surely find out themselves how the world works. Thus: acknowledge a patient's last-ditch aspirations, share those aspirations with others close to them, educate about the medical issues, and assure them their health-care team will stay the course as the tenses change.

NOT JUST THE HAND, BUT THE ARM

Because they are dolts, Edie's father responds. Put your arm down, sweetheart.

SHUT OUT OF YOUR OWN LIFE

To imagine the Minkowski Diagram, picture two funnels of time, one's tip balanced atop the other's.

Where those tips touch is your present.

The bottom funnel is your absolute past, the top your absolute future. For any event to exist in your absolute past, every observer in the universe must be able to agree that it occurred. That is, the absolute past, your absolute past, is causal, verifiable, and therefore indisputable. It leads without doubt to your thin-waisted present. From there stems without doubt a large (though not infinite) number of possible absolute futures which are also causal, verifiable, and therefore indisputable. These kissing funnels represent zones in which time moves in a straight line and motion cannot, given the universe's ordinances, exceed the speed of light.

To the left and right of those funnels of temporal certitude, however, lies what Minkowski called *absolutes Anderswo*—absolute elsewhere, absolute away, that territory which lies outside causality, predictability, and reason. Here time isn't time, chronology unthinkable, and the you of twenty years ago is, as you take the breath you are taking this instant, hugging the you of thirty years from now.

Trains arrive in stations before they have departed. Virtual particles flash in and out of existence. Fact is replaced by probability.

This is the principality where poetry was invented.

SECRET LIFE OF SOUNDWAVES

People no longer needed in Edie's life step into and close the doors of their wardrobes, and all those tiny men and women living inside the wooden radio box in her living room dwell in a mist of nickel-hued static. There they lead very pleasant lives. Of this Edie is sure. She is also sure they must always carry tiny umbrellas above their tiny heads as they traverse their tiny days. Otherwise, the static would drench their clothes and turn them into soundwaves. Sometimes they sing pretty songs. Sometimes they prattle late into the night. Edie listens to them going on and on as she meanders into sleep. She listens to her parents strike up conversations with them. That's when they are allowed to climb out of the radio box (so long as they remove their shoes and agree to act like little ladies and gentlemen) and sit around the living room balanced on chair arms as if on horses, atop books in the bookcases as if on cliffs, hanging from lamp cords like marionettes. Every night Edie asks her mother and father if she can join them. When you're a little older, they tell her. When you're a little more you.

THE INGRID, THE HANS

Although hosting a tea party for her cousins inside a hollowed-out candy cane would be quite fine, no doubt, playing by herself is even finer, because when Edie is alone those tiny beings come inside her to tell stories, and there is no difference between their thoughts and feelings and hers. But when you play with your cousins you must share your toys, which means now and then Ingrid who smells like diapers grabs porcelain Eva out of Edie's hands and Hans who smells like vinegar grabs Jaunty Schildkot Wobble Duck and Edie has to push them away and every so often they fall backward and bump their heads on the floor and detonate into wails, even though it is the parquet's fault, not Edie's, naturally, and so Edie detonates into wails, too, because how could floors be so nasty, and that's when Mommy, dishtowel in red hands, rushes into the living room, pretending to be somebody else.

WRITTEN ON YEARNING

Early on the morning of September 21, 1995, a worshipper in a New

Delhi temple pressed a spoonful of milk to the mouth of a statue of Ganesh. He was shocked to watch it vanish in the blink of an eye. Clearly the statue was alive, aware, and thirsty.

News of the miracle circled the globe.

Vehicles and pedestrian traffic around New Delhi temples gridlocked.

Six days later, a statue of the Virgin Mary in Singapore also drank milk from a spoon, and on September 28 locals offered a spoonful of alcohol to a Gandhi statue in Mumbai, which it sipped right up, causing an uncomfortable stir among devotees.

A group of scientists descended. It didn't take them long to discover, not a supernatural phenomenon, but rather a manifestation of physics. When liquid comes into contact with a statue, surface tension draws it onto the statue's exterior. Repeat the feeding motion long enough, and one can remark liquid dribbling down the statue and pooling at its base.

By October, no further reports of such wonders emerged.

NIGHT GIVES MORE THAN IT TAKES

When the bonfires show signs of succumbing to the downpour, the Berlin Fire Brigade thoughtfully shows up to help pour gasoline on the books.

TRUTH DEPENDS ON A WALK AROUND THE LAKE

Eighty-eight years later, Gordon Lish will write in a short story called "Naugahyde" the following dialogue between two characters:

We had something, she said.
He said, Don't we still?
Yes—death, she said.

CHILDREN PICKING UP THEIR OWN BONES GAME

Listen: all children are born It. There is no way around this fact. They are called Picking Up Their Own Bones. The goal of the game is to pretend they are the little boys and girls of parents who died horribly, because this will invariably be the case. If not today, then tomorrow. If not next month, then the next. So: imagine how your mother perishes. In childbirth? In flood? In a collapse of fragile arteries? A terrible automobile accident, after which she lives for seven minutes in a gale of agony? Good. And now your father. Imagine how your father succumbs. Riptide? Furnace? Slow diabetic ruination or quick slip of a chainsaw? Dreadful shredding of cancerous lungs or erosion of the kidneys? Good. And now yourself. Imagine how you will live with this information inside you. Go on. Try. This is where the game turns formidable. This is where the challenge lies. Pretend to be happy. Pretend the universe is, after all, benevolent. Say everything happens for a reason. Say oranges. Say jasmine. Say beautiful music. Pretend that it is all right to misplace your memories for a short time every day and then call those moments miracles.

TO BE SMALL AND SHINE

Out of nowhere Edie concludes she loves her father more than her mother. This throws her. All her emotions throw her. They won't stop changing. They keep walking fast as they can, getting nowhere. Edie would never tell a soul about her revelation, especially not her mother, because that wouldn't be polite, although it's true, and every so often the truth isn't polite, like that girl with the misshapen foot she plays with in the street, because the way Edie's father's shoulder feels against her cheek, the warm spicy scent of his factuality, because the scratch of his face against her skin and brown bloodstains on his apron when he steps through the door after work, hair tousled, grin aimed at her alone like an open mind, because she can sense his strength when he lifts her off the ground and she becomes giddy and weightless, because he will always protect her against teddy bears growling in closets, because he feels so utterly different from her mother and Edie always wants to do what he says to please him, because he takes her to the park Sundays and once even to the zoo where they fed peanuts to the elephants whose bristly trunks ended in the most delicate lips, because Edie tries to set the table just like her mother does, even though she hasn't quite figured out how to reach that high, and so she sets the floor instead, even though she doesn't know which way the silverware goes, but it doesn't matter, does it, no, because once upon a time her father was a student at university studying important ideas and then there was a war and the bad people won and her father was the bravest soldier in the army and that's why he can only see out of one eye since the other is sewn shut and sometimes he needs to take very long naps and sometimes enjoy his beers in spite of what Mommy says and sometimes cry out in the middle of the night *the crocodiles are coming, the crocodiles are coming, but don't be scared, sweetie, they are carrying your bad dreams away.*

SKY IS EVERYWHERE LIKE HOLY WATER

One morning in March, 2011, a devout woman cleaning a twelve-foot-tall statue of the crucified Jesus in a Catholic church in Mumbai noticed water seeping from its feet. Beside herself with joy, she spread word that a miracle was unfolding in the city's midst.

The media once again exploded into action.

Parishioners commenced collecting the holy water.

The Church of Our Lady of Velankanni promoted itself as a pilgrimage site and its coffers filled.

Sanal Edamaruku, president of the Indian Rationalist Association, turned up with an engineer in tow. They spent seventeen minutes examining the scene, after which Edamaruku went on national television to announce his findings to millions of viewers: the wall behind the statue was leaking—one could see algae growing on it. The source for the water emanating from Jesus's feet was not a marvel, but a broken sewer line.

Edamaruku was charged with blasphemy by the authorities and forced to flee to Finland to avoid persecution and arrest.

OPULENT PORTALS OF GOLDEN SUNLIGHT

Because, when thinking of her father, Edie sometimes confuses the words *you* and *me*, and when a teacup splinters across the living room parquet it does so because it wants to learn what ecstasy feels like.

SOMEONE SOMEWHERE IS TRAVELING FURIOUSLY TOWARD YOU

What beautiful blue Aryan eyes your little girl has, the barrel-chested man with the shiny face and shiny hair and rows of shiny coins pinned to his chest tells Edie's parents. Grinning, he pats her on the head, then lifts her into his embrace to deliver upon her right cheek just beside her lips an appreciative kiss.

HOW THE WORLD COLLECTS INSIDE YOU

Edie instantly dislikes everything about him.

SHRAPNEL BEINGS

Past him, she sees body parts floating free.

Broken teeth, flaring nostrils, plump tongues.

Fists hovering in mizzle and flicker.

MEMORY AS WIND

She feels her parents' emotions rushing through her.
>Her mother's indignation.
>Her father's furor.

They remind Edie of something, although she can't call up what that something is.

The rectangular-headed man's face swoops in.

Edie searches through the fog that always veils her semi-memories when she believes she is near to catching up to one.

Then she has it.

HOW FEATS BESTOW COLORS

When she is a good little girl, her mother will let Edie pick out one of her prettiest dresses to wear, her fanciest pair of high heels, and Edie will shuffle-totter through the apartment, cheeks rouged with chalk dust and water, pink lipstick more or less in the vicinity of her mouth, pink hairbows at the ends of her reddish-chestnut pigtails, thin pearl necklace dangling to her belly button, dragging her mother's purse behind her from room to room with regal flair.

DESCENT AS DESPAIR

Arms throbbing from his daughter's weight, Edie's father lowers her eighty centimeters and twelve kilograms to the cobblestones. Somehow, she now sees, she has overlooked the fact she is wearing shoes. What have her feet been doing while she wasn't paying attention? Immediately she feels unconditionally forlorn, severed from her father's gravitational field, envisions, on the far side of the leg-forest, a chain of people missing each other across the land.

WHY WE ARE UNMOVED BY ARTIFICIAL FLOWERS

Drop a wineglass from chest height and watch it burst. Gingerly dustpan up the shards. Pour them into a cardboard box. Close the box, shake it, open.

> *What do you suspect you will uncover inside?*
> The embodiment of chaos rearranged.

> *Because?*
> Because there are far more ways those shards can exist inside the

box as non-wineglass than as wineglass.

And yet?

And yet, according to physics, there is nothing preventing you from opening the box to reveal a fully regenerated wineglass awaiting you. There is simply an immensely higher probability of finding a mess of splinters than splinters' opposite. Nothing within the laws of physics says a wineglass won't appear, only that that event is statistically highly unlikely.

Therefore?

If a wineglass were to manifest, you would be unable to count its advent as any sort of miracle. It would be merely run-of-the-mill statistics at work, no matter how astounding the manifestation might seem. All you would be obliged to do is cite Littlewood's Law, repour your nightcap, and decide what you would like to read before bedtime.

WEATHER AS FORGETFULNESS

Edie can't remember what the weather was like before her mother tucked her in after dinner—the still white sky; the vivid light; the fresh green chill; the moisture saturating her room; the dankness of her pink blanket. She can't remember how, as she lay in her crib on her back, looking up at the ceiling, she noticed for the first time anomalies across it suggesting birds, or, perhaps, that someone had painted the ceiling so meticulously she can't tell the difference between it and mirage, for the more she studied the scene in the shadows, the more she could see it wasn't the ceiling she was looking at, not at all, but rather the apartment's attic through a large craggy hole, yes, and beyond the rafters into the open white sky itself. The birds—they were magpies, black heads, black tails, white breasts—the birds perched on the edge of the roof, peering down at her with their beady eyes, long stiff tail feathers alarming. Edie had the feeling they were waiting for her to slip asleep so they could plunge down to steal her breath, yet next she could make out her parents' low voices floating up the hallway, then all at once close by.

WHAT FAIRYTALES TASTE LIKE

Standing where her father has lowered her against her will, Edie senses her face reddening, tears accumulating, a whine growing at the back of her throat. She surveys her environment, weighing the pros and cons of a tantrum, whether such a decision might result in her father lifting her out of sadness once more. In the middle of that computation, her mother's chafed hand comes to rest on the back of her neck, rubbing absentmindedly, and Edie closes her eyes, lost in the *there* of it, reflecting: why is whipped cream so delicious?

SKIN HOVEL

The rectangular face swooping in at her for a kiss belongs to Hermann Göring. While Hermann understands it is Goebbels's flamboyance tonight, he has decided to attend anyway so he can revel sotto voce in this national blossoming.

Age forty, IQ 138, height 177 centimeters, well on his way to 135 kilos, instrumental in Adi's procurement of the chancellorship four months ago, Hermann is poised to become the second most powerful man in Germany.

Every one of his cells is rejoicing.

Two and a half weeks ago he created the Gestapo.

Tonight he pushes through this one body, this undifferentiated volume, absorbing its energies and messages, his spine mercilessly military-plumb.

We are reborn every day, he thinks, *by the very fact that we have refused to die.*

Six years from now Adi will declare Hermann his successor. A year after that Adi will name him Reichsmarschall des Grossdeutschen Reiches—Marshall of the Great German Empire, leader of all armed forces—not knowing, or perhaps not caring, that Hermann Ritter von Epstein, Hermann's fabulously wealthy godfather, was a Jew who had a fifteen-year affair with Hermann's mother, at one point going so far as to invite the Görings to live in one of his two small castles in Bavaria, Veldenstein, where Hermann grew up parading through the corridors dressed in the smart Boer uniform which his father had gifted him.

Epstein pulled strings to get Hermann into a good military academy, from which he graduated with distinction, and before long he was flying sorties in World War I.

But now it is this event.
The repetition of this event across the country.
The German people everywhere beginning to feel how every mind is an intention, every heart a wildfire.

Hermann was by his side when, surrounded by two thousand fledgling Nazis, Adi attempted a coup d'état in the botched Beer Hall Putsch.
Adi suffered a dislocated shoulder, was arrested for high treason and sentenced to five years in prison, although he served only eight months, during which he composed most of *Mein Kampf.*
Hermann was shot in the groin and fled to Innsbruck, where he became addicted to the morphine with which the doctors treated his pain—a lifelong habit that led to him to being institutionalized twice

in a mental hospital in Sweden, where he spent his interminable days straitjacketed in a padded cell.

Now he is pushing through this one body, this undifferentiated volume, feeling those around him falling deeper and deeper into the mystery. None of them wants war. Not yet. All they want is work, food, an outlet for their anger in the face of what their lives have become.

But give them time.

Let Hermann educate them on what they need.

Because it is always the same with dictatorships and democracies: explain to the rabble they are being threatened from within and without, denounce as unpatriotic those who would dare disagree, and people will be shrugging on their stupid uniforms and ill-fitting loyalty in the wink of a lie.

You can already see it, how tonight they have begun staring dead-eyed out of their allegiance to the flag—a concept they wouldn't be able to define, obviously, if their headstones depended on it.

One day Hermann will insist: *Every educated person is a future enemy.*

He has always been convinced beyond the shadow of a doubt he is the brightest person in any room he enters.

He is almost always right.

Two years ago his first wife, astonishing frail Carin, who had left her husband and child for him, the woman whom Hermann loved unconditionally, spectacularly, forever, died of a heart attack four days before her forty-third birthday, Hermann at her bedside.

Her death eviscerated him.

Her death enraged him.

Her death became a tapeworm living in his bowels for the rest of his life.

In her honor he commissioned a massive lodge called Carinhall on

40,000 hectares of woodland an hour's drive northeast of Berlin, where he dressed in medieval costumes for the hunting parties he hosted. Hermann and his guests found pleasure stalking the endangered species with which he stocked the place, from bison to exotic animals collected from the Warsaw Zoo, in order to recreate mythic scenes from the *Nibelungenlied*. He bedecked his fingers with rings, carried an elephant-ivory, platinum-tipped Reichmarschall baton encrusted with six hundred diamonds. He took the greatest pride in designing his own outlandish martial uniforms, which he changed into and out of four or five times a day. Chest outthrust, beaming, he wore a red Roman toga and sandals to afternoon tea.

Tonight it is the steady light rain, the smoke, the incantations, the urgencies, the blaze. It is the potencies, the propulsions, the frantic protons—and then, mid-step, Hermann catches sight of her: that little girl in her father's arms.

Veering, surrounded by his security detail of brownshirts, Hermann barges toward her.

Unlike Adi's vegetarian asceticism, which the Germans fetishize, Hermann adores extravagant cuisine and gaudy everything, reveres hyperbole as a way of moving through the world. He will come to own a ninety-foot motor yacht named after Carin and an armored train called Asien. His sleeping car will feature a bathtub, while other carriages will flaunt a photographer's darkroom, a six-bed clinic with operating theater, and a barbershop. Two freight cars will bristle with rapid-fire anti-aircraft cannons, and two flat cars will carry Hermann's fleet of American, French, and German automobiles, including his six-wheel-drive Mercedes W31 Geländewagen convertible.

I am what I have always been, he will one day submit to an interviewer at Nuremberg—*the last Renaissance man, if I may be allowed to say so.*

Ever since his days parading through those corridors in the castle Veldenstein, Hermann has believed our stories amount to traces of ourselves we leave behind when we move on.

No stories, no traces.

No traces, you might as well never have existed.

Sometimes in the insomniac hours of the night, he will bolt alert, believing Carin has just died a nightmare death beside him, and reach across the bed for her hand, relieved to find it, clasp it, cherish its presence in the darkness, only to realize it belongs to a different wife.

Hermann will marry Emmy Sonnemann, an actress who will come to be known as the First Lady of the Third Reich, a title that will chagrin Eva Braun—whom Emmy will openly detest—to no end. Emmy and Hermann will have one child, exquisite Edda, whom they will name after Mussolini's daughter, a fact Edda will deny up to the hour of her death at eighty in Munich in 2018, having never ceased defending Hermann's legacy.

The things that happened to the Jews were horrible, she will maintain, *but quite separate from my father.*

His speedy rise through the ranks of the Nazi party will be accompanied by his ever-expanding waistline. Together with his obvious drug addiction, bizarre clothes, loud self-indulgence, and strident dandyism, this will make him an easy target. Ordinary citizens to the Nazi elite will take sardonic glee in referring to him as *Der dicke Hermann*, Fat Hermann—even as he will come to show off with that distinctive smirk of his the more than four thousand pieces of priceless paintings, sculptures, jewelry, and furniture he will have looted from Jewish homes with the plan to turn Carinhall into a grand museum; even as next year he will engineer the bloodbath known as the Night of the Long Knives, during which he will sit in his Berlin villa at a large oak table in a gold-trimmed velvet chair, enjoying a good Cuban cigar, a glass of sherry, a bit of Bach, while his SS hit squads assassinate more than eighty rivals in order to consolidate his power.

Hermann knows none of this as he closes the distance between himself and that little girl, two meters, one, somehow sensing in her his own future daughter's proximity.

Only when captured by the Allies at the end of the war will Hermann be forced to detox and lose weight in preparation for his trial, where, displaying his signature wit and charm, he will be the sole accused able to bring the court to laughter several times while running circles around his American prosecutor, Supreme Court Judge Robert H. Jackson, causing Jackson at one point to throw down his headphones and stalk out of the courtroom.

I am a man who is basically opposed to atrocities or ungentlemanly actions, Hermann will tell his interviewer in Nuremberg. *In 1934, I promulgated a law against vivisection. You can see, therefore, that I disapprove of experimentation on animals.*

Found guilty of conspiracy to wage war, war crimes, and crimes against humanity, Hermann will be sentenced to hang—the means of execution afforded common criminals.

Incensed, he will demand death by firing squad.

The Allies will decline.

On October 15, 1946, two hours before he and ten other prominent Nazi military and political leaders will be scheduled to mount the thirteen steps to the gallows constructed in the prison gymnasium, Hermann, now fifty-three, will bite down on a cyanide capsule secreted in his cell. The ropes used for the hangings, it will come to light, will have been measured improperly, and come up short. Most of those sentenced will therefore die, not of a quick broken neck, but rather by strangulation lasting in some cases nearly half an hour, having first sustained bleeding head injuries from hitting the sides of the trapdoors that were cut too small.

How that capsule reached Hermann will remain a puzzle. Possibly it will have been passed along by one of the young, impressionable American guards with whom Hermann became friendly and for whom he cheerfully signed autographs. Possibly it will have been concealed all along in a jar of Nivea hand cream, which arrived in prison tucked into the luggage with which Hermann will be traveling when arrested.

In any case, on that Tuesday night in mid-October, he will lie on his back on the metal bed in his cell, blanket pulled neatly up to chest, arms visible atop the covers per penal requirements, and bite down.

Choking sounds will draw the guards over to the window in his cell door.

By the time they fumble in, Hermann's heart will have stopped and the smell of bitter almonds permeated the room.

His left eye will be squeezed shut, his right still open, as if winking a last little fuck-you at the universe.

THE LAW OF BUBBLES

I would do it all again, Sanal Edamaruku affirmed in Helsinki. *Miracles are like bubbles. You prick them and they're gone.*

GLASS MOUNTAIN

Testimony, Hume pointed out, given innate human fallibility, is a kind of evidence very likely to be in good part false. The evidence for miracles is testimony. Thus the evidence for miracles is very likely to be in good part false.

A generation earlier, the Irish rationalist John Toland noted that a belief in miracles tends to decrease as the degree of education—

which is to say the ability to contemplate critically—increases. *It is very observable*, he remarks in *Christianity Not Mysterious*, his 1696 monograph, *that the more ignorant and barbarous any People remain, you shall find 'em most abound with Tales of this nature.*

For Wittgenstein, the miraculous is a way of seeing rather than an event itself, while for the Swedish philosopher Celan Solen it is nothing more than a linguistic mistake, the remnants of a Christianity that has colonized our tongue without our being cognizant of the deed: by using words like *miracle*, we display just how little we are able to judge for ourselves, how much the history of language is committed to damaging our attempts at thought.

PERSISTENCE OF ASHES

Hermann doesn't know any of this as he stands before Edie Metzger and her parents in the steady light rain, in the toxic haze of books, in the chants that were once different people. He doesn't know that in thirteen years his corpse will be laid out haphazardly atop a trunk in the Nuremberg prison for the media to document, no one having bothered to close his right eye for him, nametag askew on chest, before what is left of him will be incinerated without ceremony and scattered on the Isar River along with the ashes of the other executed officials.

PURITY AS SCENT

All Hermann knows is the sound of his own voice saying: *What beautiful blue Aryan eyes your little girl has.*

The nearness of his future daughter.

His own hand reaching out, patting Edie—whose name he will never learn—on the head.

His strong arms commencing to lift her for an appreciative kiss upon her right cheek just beside her lips.

WOLF DREAMS (1)

Edie is not yet convinced our bodies must conform to the world and so releases a reptilian hiss.

THIS GRAMMAR OF NEGATION

She's not Aryan, snaps her father.

WOLF DREAMS (2)

Then Edie goes for his lower lip.

HOW PERSPECTIVE ARISES

She bites until she tastes, not fairytales, but blood, lets go, the comprehension arriving for the first time in her life that there are different ways of looking.

NO ESCAPING GRAVITY

Hermann yanks back, electrocuted, the comprehension arriving for the first time in his life that everything means something else.

It's just never exactly clear what that something else is.

EVERY YOU, EVERY ME

Glaring, he takes Edie in completely, smirk expanding and dissolving briefly into sneer, melting back into smirk, and, as if nothing untoward has happened, vanishing.

SONG TO SAY GOODBYE

Hermann gently passes Edie back into her shaken father's arms, turns, and barges on into the burning night.

AT THE END OF THE AGE OF WONDER

Two of Hermann's security detail stall three seconds, six, looking slack-faced from child to father to mother to child, assimilating, then hurry to catch up with their leader, who is already patting a little blond boy on the head several meters farther along.

CITY OF LUMINOUS FOG

A woman on a plane awakens from uneasy sleep as she senses the first loss of altitude.

The engines drop in tone.

Her ears pop.

A mechanical rumble shudders through her body.

She presses her forehead to the window.

Everything outside is fog the color of metallic dawn light and rain droplets beetling backward across the plastic.

Eva Braun—short curly hair, bulbous nose, surprisingly flavorless—

is on her way from Munich to join Adi for a few days in Berlin. She is twenty-three years his junior. Nine months ago, she aimed her father's pistol at her chest and fired, trying to catch Adi's attention and prove her devotion. That made them lovers. Two years from now, she will take an overdose of sleeping pills when he fails to make enough time for her in his overwrought life. That will make them inseparable. For forty hours at the end of April 1945, they will live as husband and wife.

Eva has no recollection of the former, no premonition of the latter.

Nor is she conscious that the plane she is on is this minute passing over Opernplatz on its final descent south into Tempelhof. She doesn't know about the rally, isn't cognizant that the rain down there has started to ease up, the audience to disperse into the oily fumes of factories along the Spree.

On the contrary, she leans back in her seat, wraps herself tighter in her blanket, shuts her eyes in an effort to extend her dreams a few oddnesses more, as on the ground Edie Metzger tilts back her head to search for the source of the engine drone above her, as her father annoys her hair with his enormous palm, saying *Good girl, sweetheart— you just took a bite out of the devil himself,* as her mother breaks into a short-lived, lighthearted laugh beside him.

THE MELTING FAITH GAME

Listen: only *you* are born It. There is no way around this fact. So you must step through the front door of your apartment at dinnertime after playing outside with that girl with the misshapen foot and be met, not by your parents, but three men in suits wearing gas masks. They lunge at you before you can react and that's the last thing you remember before you wake up on a rapidly melting slab of ice the size of a bed in the middle of the Mediterranean. The water around you churns with crocodiles. There may be magpies wheeling above you in the sky. There may be other children screaming and splashing in the sea around you, busy forgetting they are children. Your mother and father, cheering you on, may be rocking in a rowboat too far away to reach you in time. These additions are optional. Within reason, you may choose others. The goal of this game is to figure out how to survive a little longer (though never indefinitely) by gathering clues from the hundreds of jigsaw puzzles lying at your feet. One of them is solvable, the others not. Unfortunately, it will always take you too much time to guess which. Alarms are sounding. Everything you ever bought was broken before you bought it.

THE MUSEUM OF INTERRUPTIONS

Edie must have slid back into sleep, because when she opens her eyes she is draped over her mother's shoulder, not her father's, floating through the dimly lit streets on her way somewhere else, all the furor of tonight now in a place she has already begun to misremember. She isn't aware that her parents have crossed Unter den Linden, are crooking down ever narrower, emptier, darker lanes, shortcutting to the Friedrichstraße station to avoid the crowds. It is her heavy eyelids closing and Berlin tumbling away into the thin fragrance of her mother's rose perfume mixed with soap on the collar of her fluffy coat, as Edie wonders if maybe she really loves *her* more after all, decides she will have to weigh this question at greater length some other time, and, with her next inhalation and exhalation, losing that plan altogether, her parents' footfalls welling into everything, the melody of their words her only there.

DERIVATION OF INCONSISTENCY

In the seventeenth and eighteenth centuries, Voltaire and Spinoza argued against miracles, the very idea of which the latter described as *sheer absurdity*. Their reasoning followed essentially the same line.

Surely, they contended, we can all agree that the will of god is identical to the will of nature, because it is god in his flawlessness who created flawless nature. Yet we must consequently also agree that by definition a miracle is a violation of those laws of nature—that which god, whose will is inviolable and perfect, brought into being. Thus, the notion of a miracle is preposterous. Why would god contradict himself by violating his own omnipotence and omniscience? For kicks? In order to entertain or impress us? Persecute us for reasons unknown? Confound us because he has nothing better to do with eternity?

Shouldn't his world as we find it be sufficient to satisfy us?

Another way of putting it: what on earth would humans need miracles for? Their presence would indicate a complete lack of forethought, power, or both on the deity's part. Claiming the presence of a miracle would amount to blasphemy.

BERLIN, 2:12:07 A.M.

Next this abrupt jolt.

BERLIN, 2:12:08 A.M.

This abrupt halt.

VALLEY OF THE UNRAVELING

These two slack-faced brownshirts from Hermann's security detail standing in front of them, blocking the sidewalk.

Everything shadow, everything silence.

Moonlight blushing through clouds.

The man on the left says: Back there. That shouldn't have happened.

Edie's father weighs the words, the scene in which he participates, replies: Get the fuck out of our way.

The man on the right laughs the way an old dog clears its throat.

Look at that, Klaus, he says. The jewboy's telling us what to do.

He's giving us orders, says Klaus. Isn't that amusing?

Everyone standing still in the wet cold air shot through with the tang of oil, coal fumes, and tautness, calculating.

Edie's father says quietly: I apologize. I shouldn't have said that. I'm— It's just—

It's late, Klaus offers.

You're tired, offers Uwe.

Yes, Edie's father says, making an effort to feel marginally relieved.

Perfectly understandable, Klaus says. We might well feel the same in your shoes. It's been a long night.

I'm sorry, Edie's father says. It was stupid of me.

But you weren't sorry before, Uwe says to Edie's mother. You were laughing at us back there.

No, Edie's father says. We were—

Please, Edie's mother says.

Klaus glances over at her.

Don't talk to me, he tells her.

Everyone standing still a little longer, until Edie's father says: You don't have to do this.

Do what? Uwe asks. What do you think it is we don't have to do? He turns to Klaus: What do you think he thinks it is we don't have to do?

Please, Edie's mother repeats.

Do you understand German? Klaus asks her.

We just want to go home, Edie's father says.

To Palestine? Uwe asks. A little late for that, isn't it. We gave you kikes plenty of time. Didn't we give you plenty of time?

So I'm interested, Uwe says: which are you—deaf or dumb?

Listen, Edie's father says.

The listening train's already left the station, Klaus says.

I have some money.

Uwe grins.

Money? he says.

It's not much, Edie's father says, but—

Uwe turns to Klaus: He thinks we want his money. Jew to the bitter end.

That's amusing, Klaus says.

Then he turns to Edie's mother and says: Give us the girl.

Nobody moves.

Nobody moves some more.

Let me ask you something, says Uwe. What kind of parents are you yids anyway? What kind of manners do you teach your little monkeys?

HOW THE PHILOSOPHER PROVES THE PHILOSOPHER EXISTS (1)

To Edie's father it feels as if someone is squeezing all the air out of him.

Everything slows down.

Everything becomes restless and strained.

Edie's father can't determine anything he could do that might make these next few minutes turn out well, so he stops thinking.

HOW THE PHILOSOPHER PROVES THE PHILOSOPHER EXISTS (2)

Klaus takes a step toward Edie still half-sleeping on her mother's shoulder.

Everything slows down.

Then everything speeds up.

WORLD ARRANGING ITSELF INTO POEM

Edie's father pulls back from the scene in which he is participating and sees it with such unexpected clarity, the moon's appearance striking him as so magnificent, that it occurs to him he must be dying soon.

A HUMAN BEING TAKING THE SHAPE OF HIS CONTAINER

Not thinking, he launches his bulk at Klaus's, unaware that another of the brownshirts has come up behind him to wait for him to make just such a move.

(The third brownshirt's name is Egon. Nine years from now a housewife whose name is Arina will step out from a cupboard where she has been hiding when Egon is focused on incoming fire and ease a carving knife between his ribs during house-to-house combat in a city called Stalingrad. It will take Egon three minutes to beat Arina into another universe, twenty minutes before he joins her there.)

Before Edie's father can close the distance between Klaus and him by ten centimeters, the third brownshirt's black billy club meets the side of his head.

HOUSE OF LIGHT

The noise inside is incredible.

It arrives in the form of a bluewhite flash the breadth of the sky.

Edie's father's intended trajectory crumples into itself, his blood spattering his wife's face, the back of his daughter's head.

THE BEWILDERMENT OF LIVING

Now Edie's mother is somehow down on her hands and knees on the sidewalk beside her husband without understanding how she came to be there, dazed, mouth open and leaking fluids, thinking *where is my baby where is*—which is when she acquires another clout across the base of the skull and her world turns off.

DUMP TACKLE

Edie's father compresses all his residual energy within himself, believing for the briefest instant that we are our choices.

He grits his teeth and erupts toward Uwe's belly like a rugby player.

MISCARRIAGE AS FOOTWEAR

Egon's jackboot lunges out of nowhere and cracks into Edie's father's ribcage.

He temporarily misplaces his ability to breathe as his right cheek skids on cobblestone.

THE DENTISTRY OF ABUSE

The night becomes noiseless except for his wife's sobbing beside her husband as she spits up the blood gathering in her mouth where her two front teeth used to be.

HOW TO READ WITH YOUR NERVES

Edie remains mute and piercingly vigilant during her ride on Klaus's shoulder. He and his hulking friends smell funny and they are mean and Edie hopes she is inhabiting another dream even though she is almost certain she isn't, even though she is convinced her parents will retrieve her any second because she loves them both equally and where are they?

WHAT DO ALLEYS CONTAIN?

Uwe, Egon, Klaus, and Edie upon Klaus's shoulder duck into an alley lined with trashcans and broken brown beer bottles.

ALL TOMORROW'S PARTIES

Edie doesn't experience what comes next.

She doesn't experience what she experiences.

Klaus simply swings her off his shoulder and tucks her under his arm like a sack of cornmeal.

Above her, Klaus is huffing. She can sense her forward momentum slowing. She can hear Klaus's huff turn into a different sound, the one Schaum makes when coughing up a hairball.

Next she is on the ground and Klaus, Uwe, and Egon are bent double a few meters away, hands on knees, dismayed, their violeting faces sweaty and swollen.

That's what they are doing, it comes to Edie: they are gasping for air.

Down on all fours, Klaus looks at her with drowning eyes.

The oxygen molecules in the alley rush into a shimmery sphere near one of the dented trash cans.
Wheezing, the men struggle toward it.

Edie waits, waiting.

ALTERED CARBON, ALTERED HYDROGEN

The princess of everything doesn't experience the sensation of the stucco wall flying toward her. The electric shattering. The brusque disconnection from her life. She experiences instead the color red more vividly than she has ever experienced it before, a color that proves too much beauty can be painful. Redder than fear. Redder than fury. Red abundance rising through every realm she knows: a sea that presses against her bedroom windows, dribbles through the cracks, all at once bursts through, splashing over her crib, saturating her blanket, soaking her flannel nightie freckled with rosebuds, heaving out the door, along the hallway, picking up astonished Schaum in its hurry, blasting through the front door, waterfalling down the stairs and out into the streets, blocks away pouring through the Friedrichstraße station, reaching and swamping the park where her father and she once played, drowning the crinkly trumpeting elephants in their zoo cages, carrying off the giant hollowed-out candy cane and her shrieking cousins, soon even her memories of the winter market and the scent of her mother's coat collar and the rasp of her father's face against her skin.

It carries off everything—first Berlin, then Germany, then all Europe, the earth, the planets, everything, and before long the only thing that remains of Edie Metzger is the hole where her name used to be.

II

Love is friendship set to music.

—Jackson Pollock

No, that's not it, that's not how it happens, it's—

—because I'm here, have been for years, in the backseat of this Oldsmobile 88, top down, wind enraged, tearing along some country road at night, Jackson drunk at the wheel, Ruthie by his—

—the world all quick nervous giggles and skinfizz, the whirled world, the world like leaves spinning in a crazy autumn gust, only it's not autumn, no, that's, it's what, it's—

—August, where did the summer, nearly ten o'clock, yes, warm damp air cramped with overripe foliage, faint sea rot—

—except *here* won't fit into time—

—this brutal unsteadiness—

—Ruthie going *slow down, Jackson, honey, slow down*—

—only he won't slow down, isn't even thinking about slowing down, because he's angry, he's been angry on and off all day—

—because this should be a party, that's what he, *we should be having a goddamn party*, he's saying, because—

—because Springs, New York, is Springs, New York, because I'm here, because his wife is in Paris, because Lee won't leave him and won't stay with him, and maybe they're getting a divorce and maybe they aren't—

—because Ruthie phoned me day before yesterday, Wednesday, no, Thursday, it was Thursday, that's—

—she in the city to get away from him a few days, clear her head, inviting me out to their farmhouse on Long Island to keep her company, keep her sanity—

—she needed her best friend by her side, she said, someone to be with her, anyone that's not, could I—

—*we have this thing between us,* she telling me over the phone, *don't get me wrong, Jackson and me, we have this thing, anyone can see it—*

—*you've got to realize he's my life, sweetie, I'm everything to him, it's—*

—*that's what scares me, I've never lived with anybody else before, a man, I mean, never lived with a, not like this, the intensity of him, the endless storm of Jackson, he goes off, you'll see what I—*

—*I never know who he's—*

—*sometimes my lover sometimes my father sometimes my collaborator sometimes my little kid and I can't stand the—*

—*I don't know what to do, how to behave—*

—*I'm rambling, I know, I'm sorry, I'm rambling—*

—*please just say you'll come out for the weekend, a day or two—*

—get away from the, enjoy the farmhouse, see how I, we can swim at the beach, would you like that, the pebbled beach, Gardiners Bay, drink champagne, wouldn't that be—

—meet him, see his paintings, tell me what you—

—help me get a little perspective on everything—

—because, you know, he said he's going to divorce her, that's what he promised, he's ready, you can tell, it's taken such a long time, but he's—

—he just has to get all the finances in order, it isn't easy—

—I'm twenty-six, how did this, him forty-four, good god—

—the whole thing's mad and beautiful and unimaginable and I need to get my bearings, get a little, I don't know—

—you can help, I know you can, I'm in over my head, sweetie, I'm the first to admit it, and I love it and I hate it and say you'll come, Edith, say you will—

—because Thursday evening I'm on the phone with her like that, Ruthie's voice churning like clothes in a dryer, and Saturday morning we're boarding a train in Penn Station, me with my one tiny worn suitcase, tan, brown trim—

—everybody needs to know when she reaches out there will be someone else there to take hold—

—a couple hours later I'm there, here, in the backseat of a shiny green soft-top Oldsmobile 88 tearing down a country road like time is broken—

—I can't remember what it's supposed to—

—which way it's supposed to go or how fast—

—Ruthie saying *come on, baby, you're scaring Edith,* and for some reason I can't stop giggling, it's terrible, I'm terrified, this isn't—

—I can't stop giggling and can't stop struggling to think about anything else, about—

—how Ruthie and I go so far back, that's, yes, we're like sisters, family, and you don't let family down, do you, ever, that's what they, despite the evidence, no matter what, you—

—Ruthie making twenty-five bucks a week when we met, *twenty-five,* collecting unemployment insurance, working behind the desk at that gallery on Fifty-Sixth Street—

—all she wanted in life was to be a painter, remember, she'd do anything, that's what she—

—every day that's what she told me, *I'm going to be a painter even if it kills me*—

—how she gave off that uneasy smell, you meet it everywhere in the city, this combination of naked panic and need—

—chubby rats sliding across subway platforms and incoherence, restlessness and savage competition, Rome burning everywhere—

—once you've lived in New York every other place feels like a mistake, that's what they say, I wouldn't, I'm not—

—only all Ruthie and I can afford to do is sit around her kitchen table on Sixteenth Street and talk about someday, the next big thing, because that's all we have left to talk about, that's—

—we used to call it hope—

—the kind you don't believe in but pretend you do to make conversation and another week of nothing passes by—

—talk about makeup and movies in the scruffy fifth-floor walkup she shares with a roommate who plays cello and wears thick tortoise-rimmed glasses that make her look like a communist—

—her name, the roommate's—

—Sandra, Sandy, best scam ever—

—three or four affairs going at once, handsome guys, faithful, young, some married, who cares, you only get one life—

—when things heat up she out of the blue announcing she's pregnant, early days, no bump, no prospects—

—that's what she, turning weepy, begging them to—

—you should see how they believe without question, power of faith, that's why religion works, spooked and proud—

—coughing up the nine hundred for that trip to Havana so fast you—

—which is how she makes enough to play the cello, buy food, attend a concert now and—

—you've got to admire her, how she can turn any day into an opera—

—making believe she's tracking down the right doctor, the right contacts, arranging the travel, the buses, the flights—

—a girl's got to applaud a girl's ingenuity—

—we all find secret ways to create our own prisons, earn our own parole, run and run—

—except us—

—Ruthie and me—

—we just sit around her kitchen table, drinking cheap red wine, smoking Lucky Strikes to lose a couple pounds, talking till one in the—

—of course about men—

—about where we want to be in five years and why we won't get there and how come only other people's lives seem to make any kind of sense—

—because it was Ruthie's passion for beauty parlors, the glossy rituals, that brought us together, imagine—

—funny, the luxury of somebody lathering your hair for you, such a big deal—

—how you all of a sudden become the princess of everything—

—that indulgence of sitting under the dryer reading *Vogue* until you get bored and then basking in the application of your mascara, nothing more, just that, the feeling of—

—which somehow sets better in the heat, the mascara, who knows why—

—zero to do on a weekend afternoon save lounge around—

—and me working as the receptionist and manicurist—

—we hitting it off right away, Ruthie and me, because we knew we were sisters, family, and family never—

—you make your own, don't you, of course you do, the universe gives you one family and you spend your life making another, the version you really wanted all along—

—your own family in the end unfailingly proving a disappointment in countless ways—

—a something that went wrong at some point you never noticed until you look back and see what a bunch of smashed dishes yours is—

—so you share some strands of DNA with somebody else—

—big deal—

—me still living in Washington Heights with my fretful mother—

—she who kvetches to the ceiling at dinnertime, all nerves and disillusionment in the face of the future—

—the past—

—the present—

—a little alarmed bunny rabbit convinced any minute the sky will fall and she will die a beggar sorting through trash cans in some alley in Hoboken, her children having abandoned her to the elements and her recollections—

—my bully brother with the prolific-toothed smirk, eyes clear and cold and amber as a goat's—

—how he used to steal my allowance and spend it on root beer Dum Dums because the putz knew I wouldn't—

—how do any of us survive childhood?—

—he shoved me under the covers, refused to let me out for air, the crush, the fear, the scrabble, like your apartment building caving in on you—

—we had some good times, too—

—I'm sure of it—

—even if I can't recall with any—

—and Ruthie coming all the way from Newark because once when she was seven she read a biography of Beethoven, one of those written for kids, and on the spot decided she wanted to live an artist's life in the big city—

—the only place you can do that unless you go to Paris, she said—

—and we both Jews, her grandparents from eastern Europe, me from Germany, that's where I was, both of us growing up fatherless—

—hers sneaking away from the mess of his existence when she was a little girl, mine never making it out of the war, Berlin, the war—

—which is how we figured one night over a bottle of cheap red wine and a pack of Lucky Strikes that that was probably why we both had a thing for older men—

—Freud never leaving any of us alone for very long—

—me describing to her in detail my boss, Nicky, Nicky Nigito, what we had going—

—sweet Nicky of the five o'clock shadow at eleven in the morning, Italian biceps, knock-you-over-with-a-feather Old Spice—

—those fancy suits—

—oh my goodness—

—so what if he's married with two little brats and this beautiful wife named whatever she's named, Nancy, Nicky and Nancy, that's, yes, who if the truth be known is a very nice person—

—you only get one life—

—use it like hell—

—which is hard to admit about the wife of the man you're dating, but it's true, she is, and we get along well, even if Nicky is the only real reason I keep coming into work—

—tedium that expands in your head till you can actually feel it pushing against your brain like some damaging creature—

—you can sense your mind withering—

— a few thousand cells every hour—

—how easily your life can be duplicated, is the thing, that's what you—

—how easily you can be dead even with your eyes open—

—I don't think I ever expected better from this world, but I don't think I ever expected this, either—

—*can you hurry up with that, Edith, can you step on it a little, sugar*—

—that sham politeness you apply every morning along with your lipstick and rouge—

—or the cranky anorexic in a bleached Angie Dickinson bouffant with poodle strung out on bennies squirming under her arm—

—rat-dog's black lips pulled back in wrath at you—

—mouthful of needle-teeth six inches from your face—

—that cranky anorexic proving who's in charge, just for kicks, like it doesn't kill you a little more every day—

—just because her own life is so whatever it is—

—splintered into a thousand pieces—

—because Jackson isn't slowing down, he's speeding up, the skinfizz, the wind, how it—

—me squinting against what's to come, squinting and giggling, this new world I am, every me—

—we don't like it, all the people I'm not—

—and so night after night Ruthie and I sitting at that kitchen table—

—headlights all at once flicking off—

—road going dark before us—

—*Jackson, baby, what are you doing?*—

—night after night ventilating about how much more exciting it is to be courted by an older man—

—how they've lived a volume you can't even—

—more charming, tender, smarter, sexier, wiser, too—

—more cultivated and appreciative of you than those snot-nosed little shits in their twenties, pardon my French—

—can't even afford to treat you to a coffee and date-nut-bread sandwich at Chock Full o'Nuts—

—jeez oh man—

—telling Ruthie all about how Nicky takes me out to classy restaurants—

—everybody knows his name, *yes, Mr. Nigito, by all means, Mr. Nigito*—

—classical concerts—

—ballet—

—*ballet*—

—me, Edith Metzger from, imagine—

—we talk about the books I'm reading because he's reading them, too—

—generous, caring, funny, smart, adorable Nicky—

—the feel of him beside me in the hotel bed—

—his skin—

—those muscles—

—if he gets into an argument with somebody he never raises his voice because he can level a guy with a line—

—*you're the reason shampoo comes with instructions,* like that, such a, how can you not—

—sometimes I have second thoughts, sure I do, who doesn't—

—the specialness sometimes souring, curling up around the edges like an old paperback, it's just the way it—

—sometimes Nicky demanding too much—

—wanting my life to fit into his like a—

—but Ruthie, she can massage my worries away, remind me in that way she has how cute I am, petite, my pretty blue eyes, full lips, feathered black hair—

—how lucky any man—

—family—

—*don't waste it, sweetie,* she's saying—

—*love, no matter what the terms, no matter how differently you define it from everybody else*—

—it has its ups and downs, sure, look at Jackson and me, but you know in your bones it's its own reward—

—who cares what anybody else, how other people, that's their business, this is yours—

—so let it go, Edith, seriously, just let it go, for once in your—

—make your desires into something you can flourish inside of because listen, honey, this is the fifties, we're all writing our own screenplays now—

—Ruthie wrote hers in spades, surfacing from the Lincoln Tunnel, this twenty-six-year-old wide-eyed kid from Jersey—

—second afternoon in New York blustering into the first uptown gallery she stumbles across, right up to the first person she saw, who happens to be Audrey Flack, *Audrey Flack*, what are the—

—and Ruthie goes *excuse me, I think you might be able to help me, who are the best artists in the city right now, who should I know, in what order, would you say?* —

—without missing a beat Audrey answering *Pollock, de Kooning, Kline,* like that, *they hang out at the Cedar Bar … you know it?* —

—and Ruthie: *Can you draw me a map?* and Audrey actually takes the time to—

—and Ruthie: *thanks so much—oh, and one more thing—if I'm not, you know—where does he usually sit, Pollock, when he's there?—*

—and there she is on the corner of University Place and Eighth Street like she owns the joint—

—stepping through the door into this crowded dive, she telling me, *pea-soup green walls, cigarette haze, pong of urine seeping in from the toilet at the back—*

—people huddled four deep at a long glossy bar, poor-casual, coarse, loud, wild—

—and there I am ordering myself the cheapest whiskey, daydreaming in a booth, maybe an hour, who knows, only then the entire atmosphere around me changing—

—because there's Jackson thundering in, tired, ruined, shredded by life, pausing to look around—

—shorter than I'd imagined him, thickset, rumpled tweed jacket, no tie, wrinkled polo shirt, balding, forehead old and furrowed, beard stubbly—

—and yet the most irresistible blue eyes, I could see them from, indescribable, like yours, sweetie, just like yours, I could see them all the way from—

—you should have felt the energy he was giving off, this unbelievable aura, everyone in the place could sense it coursing through them—

—a continuous low-grade electrical current—

—and next there he is standing right in front of me, offering me a drink, G&T, I couldn't, you're new around here, aren't you, *him saying, like we'd already been introduced, like we'd already known each other for—*

—because I haven't seen you before, he's saying, tell me something interesting about yourself, *sliding into the seat across from me,* nothing about art, okay, not a fucking word about that crap, just tell me something nobody else in New York knows about you—

—like we understand each other immediately, that cliché, I know it's crazy, I know, I'm not stupid, I know it's just movies, like that, but it's not, too, if you know what I—

—all I wanted to do was tell him, what, what did I want to tell him—

—that I got his sadness—

—I'm sad in the same way—

—because it has something to do with being stuck in one body that can only occupy one place at a time—

—how our mothers' smiles were lies—

—seeing how things have turned out in your life but being unable to reach back to your younger self and explain what's going to—

—brace yourself, honey, get ready for—

—yearning to protect someone like him from the disaster of himself—

—because I know something, baby, I know you have a life vivid and complex and injured as anyone's and all I have to do is figure out the language to let you know I get that—

—you've ruined yourself, look at, you threw yourself out of the plane simply to see what falling felt like—

—I'm not looking into his eyes anymore but studying his rough hands: fingers bloated from drinking, stained yellowbrown from chain smoking—

—how he speaks with them instead of his voice—

—these exquisite ugly birds rising up around his mouth—

—half-sentences—

—approximations—

—like he's too self-conscious to finish a thought—

—like English is his third language—

—he isn't handsome, Jackson, no, not at all, don't get me wrong, sweetie, I'm not saying, he's something else—

—what's the—

—compelling—

—vital, overpowering, *this walking fire alarm, this ambulance existence—*

—and when he smiles this sorrowful aging man turns into a sweet little boy—

—next thing he's across from me in the booth holding both my hands in his, palms up, examining them like some fortuneteller—

—I'm telling him about a painting of his I saw a few years ago, the first I'd ever come across, some gallery, I forget the title, but the dynamism, how you can—

—I could feel it enter my body—

—that's what I—

—studying the canvas made me get how his heart was in this continual process of coming apart—

—which is when he interrupted saying no fucking art, please, Jesus, I've had enough—

—critics calling him Jack the Dripper like he's a joke—

—something you can look smart making fun of—

—an hour and we're standing alone in my bedroom, everything silent and dark, Sandy out for the night to a, Jackson kissing me, shy as a child, like he doesn't know exactly how to do it, like he's never done it before—

—reeking of dead alcohol and cigarettes—

—kissing me like he can't believe I could want somebody like him—

—which is when something comes over him, the alcohol, the hope, and we tumble into each other—

—become someone other than the people we had been three minutes before—

—on the other side of our skin this new dimension widening—

—and when I open my eyes again he's sleeping with me in my disarrayed bed, fetal, backed against me, snoring, my arms around his thick waist, me thinking I'm snuggled tight against the devil himself—

—a fool and a madman and a cowboy and a saint—

—I have absolutely no idea who I'm holding—

—it's Thursday evening and I'm on the phone with Ruthie and next it's early Saturday morning, today, and we're on the train together to Long Island, she already exhausted by what awaits her—

—forehead pressed against window—

—wishing a nap upon herself—

—me reading that new Pearl S. Buck novel about the last empress of China, it's hard to, it goes on and on, all those paragraphs, gray, but everyone's talking about it—

—it's the new Pearl S. Buck novel and then it's Ruthie and me stepping down off the train into this staggering blue day at that cute East Hampton depot, red brick, green trim—

—me holding my suitcase, a few changes of summer clothes, my swimsuit, makeup, hairbrush, toothbrush, toothpaste, deodorant, perfume—

—the Oldsmobile already in the parking lot, top down, engine idling, Jackson in the process of climbing out to fetch our bags—

—this film of grogginess surrounding him—

—like he fought his way up from sleep ten minutes ago—

—disheveled, sullen, face spoiled by loneliness—

—shuffling toward us expressionless—

—what's the word—

—*empty*—

—Jackson empty—

—Ruthie and him exchanging kisses like it's some kind of chronic duty—

—and when she tries introducing me to him all he does is grunt—

—me holding out my hand to shake and him shuffling right by, aiming for the car, carrying our bags and his pointlessness—

—throwing the suitcases in the trunk—

—slamming it down—

—which is when it hits me that Ruthie never told him I was coming along, she's springing me on him like some kind of gag gift, I didn't—

—I've been expecting some big-deal artist, who wouldn't, suave, masculine, some pure embodiment of intuitive genius, because the newspapers, because Ruthie's passion—

—only all I meet is her embarrassment—

—she's worked so hard to look fresh for him, peppy, merry, this lovely white summer dress speckled with rosebuds—

—and there we are already having run out of anything to say to each other—

—the three of us squeezing into the front seat, me pressed against the passenger door, armrest jabbing my elbow, Ruthie leaning against Jackson, counterfeiting things—

—he lighting up and me embarrassed for her embarrassment because the sunshine has turned repulsive—

—this dreadful lemon sky—

—only she refuses to drop her smile, devotes her whole being to plowing on with her feigned good cheer, it's—

—we assume we're on our way to the farmhouse—

—that was the plan, we all knew that was the plan, though as soon as he can Jackson pulls off the road and into the parking lot of some crummy redbrick bar—

—Cavagnaro's—

—eleven in the morning—

—*eleven*—

—Ruthie and I all nicely dressed, just in from the city, Jackson deliberately baiting her, trying to mortify me, except I'm not here for him—

—everybody needs to know when she reaches out—

—that's just what you—

—Ruthie going, *why are we stopping, honey, I thought we were*—

—and him cutting her off: *there's nothing to drink at home, I want a drink, why should that be such a big*—

—the second you walk in you can smell this is where the defeated go, the ones who don't own the fancy homes around here but work for those who do—

—the pool cleaners, the lobster fisherman, the drivers, the maids, the handymen who never seem able to locate enough work to make ends meet—

—gloom the sole lighting—

—mildew and discouragement—

—she choosing a booth away from the—

—the place already hot and thick, Ruthie and I ordering coffees, black, Jackson a cold bottle of Schlitz—

—I don't know how I'm supposed to—

—I become *neutral* is the—

—the three of us sitting there staring down at our drinks—

—which puts me in mind of how many times we die over the course of one lifetime before we die—

—how we make believe each of those deaths is really something else—

—we can try to become Buddhists like all those ridiculous beatniks down in the Village—

—making believe having sex with other men and wolfing peyote and writing nuts poetry is what Buddha had in mind when he took his seat underneath the whatever kind of tree that was—

—nirvana another kind of death, I suppose—

—it's so funny, funny and pathetic, like Christ and *Cosmopolitan* and General Motors, though no matter how you cut it, it all boils down to dying—

—sometimes in a big way, sometimes in a way that completely

demolishes your soul, and sometimes in a small way, like midges delivering hurt across your body every—

—like this, here, this booth, this charged hush as if waiting for something to blow up while the bartender chatters with the drunks and my best friend stares into her coffee cup as if it were a gateway to some better reality—

—tendons in her neck stiff as crowbars—

—that smile fixed on her face the most joyless, stubborn, and suffering thing I've ever seen—

—*let's go*, she says out of nowhere, bright, bubbly, fake as Formica, *come on, honey, let's go home, I want to take a shower, change—Edith, too … right sweetie? —*

—*we want to enjoy the day, it's steaming in here and we were sitting on that stupid train for—*

—*yeah, sure,* Jackson saying, *sure, lemme just order another beer here—*

—which he does, which means we have to watch him drink it, which means taking a sip, staring down at the table, taking another, like that, sometimes closing his eyes and resting his cheek on his fist so long I can't figure out if he's asleep or—

—watching him smoke two more cigarettes—

—prove how well he can buddy up to the bartender, this skeletal-faced guy with long, slicked-back gray hair and a gold front tooth on the left and no tooth at all on the right—

—you know he smells like month-old sheets—

—I'm sorry but you know it—

—and those three drunks bent low over the counter as if listening to its cryptic communiques, already having departed our solar system for the day—

—which is when time begins stretching out in my head like desolation, debris accruing, you can taste it perforating our thoughts and speech—

—imagining something—

—anything—

—holding hands with Nicky, that's, our table by the stage in the Village Vanguard, him teaching me before the lights go down how to inhale the aroma coming off your scotch before putting your lips to the—

—what refinement looks like—

—how did we get—

—what the signal? what the noise?—

—the Oldsmobile wide and long as a battleship rolling past small farmhouses with gray weathered shingles and peeling black shutters—

—black and white cows paused in fields the color of lush ferns, heads raised, chewing stupidly—

—our motion clearing my thoughts, the fresh air, the damp sun-warmth, Jackson reaching over and flipping on the radio—

—Duke Ellington waking up in the middle of *Passion Flower*—

—the slow piano—

—the honeyed alto sax—

—floating down a country road floating free of time—

—and before you know it crunching to a stop in a gravel driveway—

—Jackson's two-story dark-gray beat-up wood-frame house—

—two towering silver maples sheltering it, sprawling cherry tree, boulders growing out of long grass—

—Ruthie explaining to me as we stroll across the yard, Jackson maneuvering ahead of us with our suitcases, the place built in the 1870s—

—Lee and he paid five thousand dollars for it, *five thousand*, borrowed, Peggy Guggenheim, naturally, Jackson's default being the edge of financial ruin—

—not even heating back then—

—not even an indoor toilet—

—*but look, sweetie,* she saying as we sweep through the front door—

—*look, isn't it fabulous?*—

—and everywhere inside white light, white walls, green plants—

—shelves lined with jazz records—

—chunks of driftwood gnarled on the coffee table, atop wobbly stacks of books, and on the walls Jackson's paintings: immense, glorious, staggering, awash in restless vigor—

—yet how can you not help noticing the greasy pots and dishes and oily glasses and silverware batched in the sink, scattered along the counter—

—and nothing by *her* anywhere, by Lee, how can you not help, not one piece, that's—

—which is when it strikes me Ruthie must have taken them all down, rearranged herself into these walls—

—Jackson must have let her—

—because Ruthie is Ruthie—

—Jackson, Jackson—

—because she is nothing if not ambitious, competitive, endlessly taking stock—

—*we're all writing our own screenplays now*—

—in the midst of that she scooping up my right hand and leading me upstairs to my room—

—which is Lee's room, the one she has all to herself when she's here, some time away from him, studio and stability—

—the surfaces covered with shells harvested on their beach walks—

—scallops, yellow jingles, whelks—

—*slow down*, Ruthie saying from the front seat with greater determination now, *why are you doing this, honey*, headlights off, wind enraged, car plunging through black—

—which is when I shut my eyes and sense myself rising, levitating out of my seat, abandoning century—

—somewhere my giggles falling away behind me, replaced by a low whine growing in the back of my throat, nobody else can hear—

—but I'm also unpacking in Lee's room, hanging my clothes, freshening up, heading downstairs in this adorable light-blue cotton sundress, ruched bust, white polka dots, tiered skirt, Nicky's favorite—

—Ruthie already having begun cleaning up the counter after making us lunch—

—tuna salad, cheese, iced coffee—

—Jackson somehow all at once a different creature, I don't, wide welcoming little-boy smile, realizing for the first time I'm here too, turning to me at the table as we take our seats and asking *so what are you involved with, Edith?*—

—his hands reaching out for both of mine, somber, tender, looking me directly in the eyes, squeezing gently, saying *let me feel your tragedies*—

—a softening, a mischievous grin, *you know what,* he saying, *we've got to celebrate Ruthie's homecoming, your visit, it's time for a festival, don't you think, look at us*—

—*what a great day we've got stretching out ahead of us*—

—*what do you say we*—

—pushing back from the, disappearing, returning with a bottle of gin—

—at the counter he makes us all G&Ts jammed with ice shards—

—a toast in my—

—and then we're laughing, Ruthie and Jackson telling dumb jokes, he announcing after a while *okay, come on, bring your glasses with you, I want to show you around outside, Edith, prove to you how this is the best afternoon ever*—

—out the back door, lawn sloping down to dense salt marshes, blue herons wading, an osprey hovering, cedar groves on the horizon—

—the three of us there lingering, icy drinks in hand, condensation wet on our fingers—

—and me so relieved this afternoon has resolved into itself—

—the one we were supposed to be inhabiting—

—Jackson just this easygoing guy, enlivened—

—you can feel the tension evaporating off Ruthie like perspiration as he points out the spot in the heavy brush where he regularly catches sight of a family of red foxes—

—asking us both to bring our free hands up to cover our eyes—

—*there you go, I'll do it, too, like this, okay, just listen*—

—*take in a breath and just listen, take it all*—

—wow ... wow ... wow—

—can you feel this?—

—can you feel where we are?—

—and he's right, it is, we can, we didn't know what happiness was and now we do—

—we're congratulating each other we're still here—

—we'll always remember the three of us poised like this—

—after a while like that we make our way back to the farmhouse to shower and get into our swimsuits, Ruthie a black one-piece, mine white covered with large red polka dots and perhaps a bit more revealing than—

—Nicky—

—Jackson fixing us another round—

—we returning to the lawn, leaning back in the grass beneath the cherry tree, lazy, talking about nothing—

—relishing the absolute nothingness of it—

—next thing he's heading back toward the house, shuffle vanished at some point along the, that's, I hadn't, he's almost graceful—

—he hardly ate a bite for lunch, merely picked at a slice of cheese, worked his gin and cigarette, yet it's brought him back to life—

—Ruthie's home—

—everything's okay now—

—and a minute later here he comes, camera in hand—

—asking me if I wouldn't mind snapping a couple shots of them—

—what the three of us have found together—

—he stages the scene, sitting on a boulder hunched forward slightly in his striped short-sleeve sailor shirt, khakis, brown loafers, no socks, chest hollowed out, left leg bent at the knee, right stretched almost straight in front of him—

—such a grin, hard to believe, yet those eyes puffy, squinting to locate the camera, locate the world outside himself—

—Jackson here and not here at the same—

—you can tell he's trying to talk himself into the joy he should be feeling—

—except it doesn't matter—

—Jackson sheepishly glad to be where he is, just this and this and this, calling Ruthie over, she snuggling close with that insistent affection of hers, willing her love into the moment—

—draping her right leg over his lap, legs spread a bit more than strictly, left bent out to the side and behind her for support, both arms wrapped around Jackson's left biceps—

—steadying herself—

—that's what she's—

—Jackson's right hand beneath her thigh—

—left gripping her knee—

—claiming her—

—you can see she wants the picture to look one way, but it has come to look another, how there's something strained in their, clumsy, lopsided, this pair of entangled marionettes—

—yet Ruthie smiling proudly, convinced it's all hers now—

—you can make it out in her eyes through the lens—

—*all this, all this, all this*—

—so I count back from three to one and click—

—freeze how they want other people to see them—

—holding each other a bit too urgently—

—shot through with expectation, that's what they're, yes, an entire lifetime in a single—

—how deep the surfaces are—

—and so the image happens—

—and so the instant turns into a tiny square of film—

—and with that I see my chance, ask if it might be possible to visit Jackson's studio out in the converted barn, that's—

—I understand completely if not, of course—

—but it would be such an honor if—

—which sends Jackson hurrying back into the house for another drink and Ruthie and me on our way across the lawn—

—me telling her what I've been wanting to since I arrived, how I understand everything now, the way she feels about him, his complicated grief, openness, vulnerability, bullish self-absorption—

—how sorrow forms part of his sense of love—

—have you *seen* the way he looks at you when you're looking somewhere else, me telling her as we, the way he waits for you to talk so he can hear your voice—

—you can tell with every gesture how much he adores you—

—how frightened he is you'll leave him someday for somebody else—

—I didn't think I would, but I really *like* him, me saying—

—I'm so moved by how clear it is you two have been waiting for each other, how you'll be together until the end of your lives—

—and with that we step through a door into a tabernacle of light and color and I come up short—

—because the way sunshine floods through the overhead skylight across his unstretched canvases tacked to the walls, across the floor, his huge brushes, turkey basters, sticks lying tarry everywhere—

—on some paintings he has sprinkled sand, *sand*, who would have, added these bits of string, these nails, cigarette butts, keys, it's unbelievable, I don't—

—he's made painting into something more than itself—

—a category of sculpture—

—his footprints petrified in thick black splashes dried across wooden planks—

—everything covered in Jackson—

—Jackson rhythms, Jackson vitality, Jackson anguish—

—there's so much of him in him—

—you sense all that weight he has to carry and it crushes you—

—and so you ask Ruthie where his sadness and rage go when he's done with them for the day, what did they give him when they were with him, what does being done with them mean when he is never really done with them—

—and first thing you want to do upon entering this space is leave it, return to the farmhouse, find him and put your arms around him and tell him it's okay, Jackson, everything's okay—

—ask him how do you possibly survive from one day to the next?—

—which is when I feel the gin beginning to glow in my veins, hear myself telling Ruthie things I've never told anyone, not even Nicky—

—things about my childhood that seems like someone else's—

—how could I possibly have been that little girl and this woman, standing *here* after standing *there*, it doesn't, no, there are just too many events crowded into each of us—

—the blue movies of memory—

—the burning resin—

—I know people are good at forgetting, you see it all the, except we simply can't forget enough, can we, no matter how hard we—

—that's in his work, too—

—Ruthie's hugging me because she sees what I'm seeing, too, and she feels so good against me and I don't ever want her to—

—whispering into my ear—

—what is she whispering—

—she's whispering it's time to go back, sweetie, we need to get ready for the beach, doesn't that sound nice, a little swim before dinner—

—and we're crossing the yard in the opposite direction, arms around each other's waists, salt marsh scents, wilting grass, muggy sun—

—this is what you feel like when you're new—

—*it's what his paintings do to everyone,* she saying as we, *somehow they open you and wreck you, otherwise you're not paying attention*—

—*you're just passing by them on the way to somebody else's in some gallery*—

—*they make you want to save him*—

—she's speaking quickly, like she needs to tell me everything about her life in the next thirty feet—

—how last month he was able to get them tickets to *Waiting for Godot*, middle orchestra after a romantic dinner, only something imploded when the play started—

—every line made him wince—

—every phrase came in at him like a mortar dropping from the sky—

—and when Alvin Epstein stepped onto the stage as Lucky, long white frazzled hair, bowler, beaten, Jackson began to cry—

—softly at first, but then he couldn't stop himself, it came harder and harder, until he was heaving in his seat, everyone turning to see what this grown man—

—so loud people actually started to shush us—

—in the end we were forced to get up, excuse ourselves all the way down the aisle—

—the looks on their faces—

—I couldn't bear it—

—out of the theater, back to my apartment—

—it was—

—he's that man, Edith, and the one who in the middle of this fight we were having about him pretending in public I'm a stranger, he slapped me across the face, I didn't even, no warning, the unmitigated shock of it, the

humiliation and fury—

—followed by days trying to make it up to me, ripped down to the bone, despising himself, we don't, you know, not anymore, he can't, the alcohol, sweetie, it doesn't matter, it really doesn't—

—he starting to show me how what Lee and he have isn't so much love as accommodation—

—an unspoken pact—

—but then she came across my white scarf beneath the seat in the car last month and detonated on the spot—

—insulted, smashed—

—he told her everything, somehow thinking it would quiet her down, which of course it didn't, how could he even—

—Lee demanding he make a choice, her or me—

—make a choice or she would divorce him, break him, destroy his life—

—who would take care of him then, who—

—he still tells me Lee will come around, he believes it, he does, he says she will learn to act like an adult, that's what he says, Lee has had it her way for so long, he says, and now it's his turn to get what he—

—but all those Jacksons—

—I couldn't explain it until you were here—

—you had to see for—

—*wait*, she says, walking into the house, the Ruthie who was just speaking merging into another as she opens the screen door, phony smile sliding back into place, that miserable hopefulness she keeps wrapped around her like chain mail—

—leaving me in the living room while she strikes out in search of him upstairs, reappearing a few minutes later, *he was sleeping, he's groggy, waking up but groggy, a nap, he'll be down in a, and then we're off*—

—only we're not off, half an hour wears away and Ruthie climbs the stairs again, more hesitant this time, braced against the, me browsing the records lining the shelves, Louis Armstrong, Count Basie, Fats Waller—

—plucking one at random, studying the images on the sleeve, reading the, slipping it back, plucking another—

—considering how they're part of Jackson's paintings, too, these albums, this music—

—jazz become visual improvisation, propulsive syncopation—

—energized and injured, that's how Ruthie says it—

—and here I am, standing in their living room, in his, finally catching on, you can hear his paintings as well as see them, the sound nearly too bright, the splatters nearly too loud, the force of his body roiling through them—

—until there's a clump on the stairs and I look up and there they are, Jackson first, Ruthie behind—

—he's still woozy, he's stopped seeing me again, stopped registering the house he's shuffling through, like some old homeless guy searching out a park bench—

—making himself another drink at the counter, bleary, staring at the floorboards three feet in front of him—

—one minute, seven—

—the day frozen as we watch him—

—at last shuffling over to the fridge, G&T in hand, wordless, extracting three steaks on a plate, shuffling out to the grill on the porch—

—Ruthie's eyes meeting mine as he passes us, me smiling, what else can, our eyes meeting like that, and then out of nowhere she shrugs like *what can you do?*, crosses to the stereo, puts on Billie Holiday, pleading with someone somewhere to send back her man, all that weariness, all that unhurried regret—

—which for some reason as I place the silverware puts me in mind of how a tiny mayfly with its long thin gold-green tail and transparent triangular wings settled on the tabletop next to my plate last week while I was taking lunch at the back of the salon—

—where did it, male, yes, adult females living less than five minutes, *five minutes*, that's what my mother—

—it must have been a male in the process of, listless, unmoving—

—I simply watched it as I ate, felt the need to keep him company, just let him know something living was sharing his conclusion—

—Jackson banging through the screen door, steaks crackling, an easiness suffusing him, the drink having helped land him back into himself, and there we are, the three of us, an improvised family sitting around the dinner table, Billie replaced by Thelonious—

—Ruthie sipping red wine, telling Jackson the story about how we first met, he curious, focused, asking for details, what we were wearing, what the weather was like, how much does a perm cost anyway—

—and stepping onto the porch painted white beneath the silver maples to smoke and watch the light going metallic around us—

—Ruthie and me with our black coffees, Jackson a beer, deciding how we might spend our evening, he revealing the invitation he received yesterday from Ossorio, Alfonso Ossorio, the rich poofter artist and collector, heir to some Filipino sugar plantation fortune, Jackson's buddy, patron, I hadn't heard of—

—a benefit concert at his place, The Creeks, old Herter estate, forty rooms in a Mediterranean villa right down on the water, flower terraces out front, Persian garden in back—

—*it's spectacular*, Ruthie saying, delighted, *so damn classy, let's go, honey, can we?, can we?, that'll be our party, we can dance, it'll be a kick*—

—*good god, no*, Jackson saying, the dark reentering him, *I don't want to see anyone, holy christ, all those humans, I can't take the, all that pretension and noise concentrated in one room, what a fucking, let's just stay here and watch TV, you can make us some popcorn, maybe there's a movie on, doesn't that sound*—

—they mounting a seesaw, Jackson remarking if Ruthie wants to go so bad he'll go, naturally he'll go, sure, he loves her, what did she, he'll do anything for her, he wants to make her—

—she hearing what he's saying behind what he's saying and *no, no, it's*

*okay, honey, seriously, we can just stay here and host our own little party
with each other—*

—a switchback, her tone ratcheting up, I've never heard—

—then this sharp knife entering her voice, *you don't talk to me when
we're out anyway, you're too embarrassed, always goddamn protecting Lee,
you just flirt with the other girls … it doesn't matter, forget it, let's just stay
here*—

—and Jackson all at once empty again, expressionless, taking in Ruthie's
words, letting each fist of them hit him in the chest, turning to me as if
Ruthie hasn't spoken, as if she isn't even there anymore, asking politely
what I'd like to do—

—*whatever is fine,* me saying, neutral, *I'm just glad to*—

—the conversation unwinding like that over the next I don't know how
long—

—one forever followed by another—

—me even assuming we've left the subject only for it to return ten
minutes later, veer away again, return—

—the evening becoming an ache inside me—

—Jackson finally raising his head and declaring *okay, it's settled, we're
going,* those exquisite ugly birds rising up around his mouth, he rising
with them, going inside to call Alfonso, let him know we're on our
way—

—you can hear him slurring, speaking too loudly, then back with
a fresh G&T in hand, condensation spidering down the, saying *it's*

almost nine, music begins at ten, we've got to get a move on, let's ... this'll be fun ... it'll be totally radioactive—

—chugging the rest of his drink as he moves toward the car—

—Ruthie and I holding back a couple minutes to freshen up, me asking her side by side at the bathroom mirror *do you think he's all right, you know, how he's been—*

—and Ruthie laughing at me, giving me a little hug, *oh, sweetie, don't you worry about him one bit, he's a great driver, he's fine, he can hold his, you'll see, we'll stop somewhere on the way and get some food in him—*

—and next—

—how did we get here?—

—the signal—

—the noise—

—and next we're packed into the front seat of the Oldsmobile, top down, on our way to The Creeks, excited, nervous, I've never been to something like, a *mansion*—

—the ride lowkey, comfortable, night settling in around us—

—Jackson awake, attentive—

—it dawning on me as we roll along that I've been worrying about nothing all day, look at us, I'm a fool, Ruthie's right, we're out for a nice, that's all, yes, en route to a party, what could possibly be—

—which is when I find myself closing my eyes, letting my body little by little slacken into the specialness that's arriving from all directions—

—the lavish fragrances—

—how can we bear being surrounded our whole lives long by all our dead selves—

—I see why our minds gave us the power to bury them—

—except that's when it—

—I sense something off—

—the car has what, has started slowing down, that's, the how, the why, my eyes opening to discover us weaving side to side as we crawl along, the Oldsmobile decelerating—

—me at once wide awake—

—Jackson's head bobbing, lips parted as if about to speak—

—he's suddenly struggling to stay awake—

—Ruthie's spine frightening straight—

—she reaches out, palming his shoulder, shaking lightly as we sway through town from one side of the main street to the other—

—thank goodness there aren't any other—

—on the far side rolling to a complete stop at a fork in the—

—and next thing nothing, just us sitting there, engine idling, crickets shrilling, apprehension skittering through me like a hundred beetles revealed to daylight—

—Jackson slumped at the wheel, face pasty—

—Ruthie and me feeling him failing us in various ways—

—*what's the matter*, Ruthie asking at last, gently, *are you all right, honey? Jackson? what's the*—

—*yeah, yeah,* him saying, voice gummy, *I just wanna to stop for a second, I, um, just*—

—while he's speaking headlights creep up to a stop behind us—

—a police car, that's, a police car, the driver's door already swinging open—

—jelly-belly cop extricating himself, stiff, taking his time to stretch his lower back before strolling up to Jackson's side, scanning him, us, you make out recognition emerging across his features—

—*good evening*, the cop says, *anything the matter, Mr. Pollock?*—

—and with that Jackson performs a magic trick, it's incredible, he returns to this spot, this hour, his speech clear and firm, *hey, Howard, how's it going? no, no, we were just talking, trying to work out what the heck we want to do with the rest of our evening, you know how it*—

—Jackson shamming light laughter—

—those two launching into a chummy conversation about wives and dogs and summer heat, the party at Alfonso's, the breakfast menu at the general store—

—I can sense how tightness is everywhere inside Ruthie as she gauges our circumstances, figuring, yet you can tell Jackson knows exactly what he's, we're in good, he's guiding us through the risks with grace, having done it so many times before he makes it look—

—before long the conversation winding down—

—before long over—

—the two of them shaking hands—

—Howard wishing us all a good rest of the—

—and we're off, cautiously pulling onto the road in front of Howard's brash headlights, Jackson maneuvering carefully until the police car turns onto another road—

—and when we come across a bar, the Cottage Inn, a burger, a plate of fries, burnt coffee, anything to bring him back—

—in the parking lot he fumbling, trying to free himself from the, each movement deciphering a tangled line of trigonometry—

—Jackson this deep-sea diver in a bulky suit—

—he holds onto the door—

—pushing himself up slowly—

—one step after another in lead boots—

—wobble-shuffling toward a phonebooth outside the—

—mumbling to himself as he—

—methodically dialing The Creeks to tell Alfonso we'll be a little late, we need to pick up a bite, it's been a long—

—but Alfonso can't come to the phone right now the maid must be telling him on the other end of the line, he's already introducing the musicians, she'll give him the message—

—because when he hangs up Jackson shouts *shit, we don't have time for, we've got to get moving or we'll miss the concert, you wanted to go and by god we're—*

—I look at myself getting out, putting the car between him and me, telling Ruthie still in the front seat *I'm not going, I'm sorry, he's loaded, he doesn't—*

—*I'm calling a cab, Ruthie, we need help, we need—*

—even as Jackson thunks in behind the wheel, yanks shut the door, seals himself in an airtight chamber apart from the facts, chin sunk to chest—

—then passes out, just like that—

—only to wake with a jerk five seconds later, muttering *I don't feel so … I'm not so sure we should … I think … I think—*

—he opens the car door a few inches and throws up, long shiny strings, some splashing across the gravel, some down the side of his seat, and passes out again, breathing wet, fitful, Ruthie beside him, arm around his shoulders, cradling him against—

—comforting him like her own child though you can see she's computing, coming undone inside, we're stranded, we're—

—I try not to, but can't help it, everything's gotten so out of hand, I start to cry—

—feeling like someone who's never skied at the top of a steep run—

—*I'm sorry*, I say, *can't you just*—

—Jackson flinching alive, startled to find himself here—

—he bursts into consciousness shot through with rage, glaring at Ruthie but seeing *her*, wrenching away, shouting *get that bitch back in here Lee or we're not going anywhere, Jesus Christ, Jesus fucking CHRIST, I'm FINE, I just needed a little*—

—and to me *get in the goddamn CAR, Ruth, GET, IN, THE, CAR, NOW*—

—me standing there in the parking lot like some idiot, crying and wiping my nose with the back of my hand because there's nothing else to wipe it with—

—Ruthie saying, her voice nourishment, *come on, sweetie, it's okay, everything's going to be okay, really, just get in the car and we'll go home, I promise, you get in and we'll go straight back to the house, right, Jackson?*—

—*you drive, Ruthie*, me saying, *I don't want to be in the car if*—

—and she *oh, sweetie, I can't drive, you know that, I don't know how, I'm a city girl, just get in the car and we'll*—

—only you can hear something invading her when I don't move, something—

—*COME! ON!*, she flaring, *good god, get in the goddamned CAR, Edith, or we're just going to sit around here all fucking night, is that what you want, crapping up the whole evening for the rest of us, this is RIDICULOUS, he's fine, stop making such a goddamn fuss and GET! IN! THE! FUCKING! CAR!*—

—and there I am alone, snotting all over myself, cars crammed in at all angles around us, how did this, and look at me, me watching myself simply give up, give in, pushing and pushing and then buckling—

—sometimes there're just too many voices to fight at once—

—so I do what Ruthie orders, her tone, the color of it, its grim anger hustling me back—

—even as I hear myself asking again *you promise, Ruthie? you promise we're going straight home?*—

—Ruthie saying *yeah, yeah, sure, take it easy, just GET IN, we're not going to any goddamn party, tonight's done*—

—I can't believe how merciless—

—I step up into the back, all the way over, as far away from him as possible, wanting to trust someone—

—my hands comforting each other in my lap like a pair of blind kittens—

—we three sitting still for a long time in this blaring silence, this electric static, which is when—

—which is when he does it—

—Jackson jamming the accelerator to the floor, gravel spewing out behind us, tires grinding down into pebbles for purchase, he as shocked as Ruthie and me by the choices his body is making—

—the Oldsmobile fishtailing onto the main road, hurling toward the, how did we, into the enraged wind, into the air dense with moist leaves and sea rot—

—me giggling, appalled at the noise of myself, I don't—

—and so I do the only thing I—

—I imagine the pink marzipan Glücksschwein, the lucky pig, yes, extended toward me in my mother's cracked palm on Christmas morning—

—our Washington Heights apartment, last night's cabbage tanging the air—

—just the pink pig, the palm, my mother's distant cousins hanging shadowy in the background—

—they helped us when we, the affidavits, three years' wait, Roosevelt doing all he could to keep us out, saying we should stop with the Jew sob stuff—

—my mother's distant cousins crowded side by side on our swaybacked secondhand couch, washed-out maroon, velvet sheen, I forget their, my relatives, how could that—

—they lived one floor above us—

—took care of us when we—

—everybody admiring me in my new bunny suit—

—I'm modeling it before them, hands curled paw-ish to my chest—

—my mother having sewn pink socks onto my pink pajamas, pink floppy washcloth-ears onto my pink hood—

—my one and only present this year and the best ever—

—me soft and safe and proud inside—

—my mother having tested out her new skills as seamstress because those were the only skills she could carry with her across the—

—she, my brother, and I disembarking amid a seethe of us with nothing but those and that single suitcase between us, the one now yawning on a chair upstairs in Lee's room, tan, brown trim—

—because that year there was no tree, no candles, nothing fancy, it didn't, precisely one gift apiece, and—

—the pink marzipan lucky pig extended in my mother's cracked palm while her oldest cousin—

—what can I recall about him: these lilac lips moving amid a thorny gray outbreak of beard—

—he telling us about how in the Middle Ages farmers with fertile swine were considered successful, the swine themselves thereby growing into signs of prosperity, even today when leave-taking you can sometimes hear Germans wish you *Schwein gehabt*—

—*have a pig*, may good fortune be with you—

—because one pig could see a whole family through a harsh—

—my mother's cousin explaining, teaching me without teaching me how to become more goy—

—we were practicing namelessness—

—because if you can't be seen you can't be—

—the pig wore a green marzipan four-leaf clover on its green marzipan collar because, my mother's cousin explaining, that's all Eve could secret out of the Garden of Eden when god deported *her*—

—four-leaf clover in her tight sweaty fist—

—just like you and your small suitcase, my mother's cousin explaining—

—a little sliver of paradise in our fumbled world—

—tasting heaven once a year—

—my giggles modifying into low moans and those low moans into a Christmas song, *stille Nacht, heilige Nacht*, the way we learned to—

—because I don't know how to hear this other thing reeling around me—

—how the skin goes away so quickly—

—I'm thinking *please give me more than this night please* as I rise, stand shakily, gripping the back of the front seat for balance—

—mouth opening—

—a voice I recognize as my own chanting *stop the car! let me out! stop the car! let me out!*—

—yet he doesn't even slow down, just flicks the headlights off, flicks the headlights on, interested to see what will happen—

—what creation might look like under different circumstances—

—and behind my voice Ruthie's, her hair deranged in the wind, *shut up shut up shut up and sit the fuck DOWN! you're making everything worse!*—

—*SIT!*—

—*DOWN!*—

—her words impelling Jackson to push the car faster along a straight stretch of deserted road unfolding before us—

—lights on, lights off—

—lost in delirious speed—

—our galaxy finally having left him alone—

—*don't do this, honey, please, don't, please,* Ruthie pleading—

—only he has already deserted us—

—leaning forward into the speed, shoulders hunched against the, trying to lift off the runway into another more breathtaking realm—

—eyes all at once wide open—

—me standing behind Ruthie, faltering, shrieking *LET! ME! OUT!*—

—shocked to watch the me of me trying to climb over the side of car—

—devoted to abandoning this disarray—

—the velocity storm trying to push me back down—

—and the straightaway falling behind us, the road curving left, concrete to oil-black asphalt, the *whomp*, the car bottoming hard, jumping the crown—

—a sharp shove right—

—the me of me thrown sideways across the backseat—

—tires catching soft shoulder in an outburst of gravel and dirt—

—and Jackson yanking the wheel too hard, overcompensating, the Oldsmobile lunging into brush, swerving on and off the edge of the—

—one hundred feet, one-fifty, trees flinging past—

—he clenching the steering wheel as if the horns of a—

—in awe before this terminal eccentricity—

—and then—

—how did?—

—he just—

—Jackson just lets go—

—the ugly birds rising up around his mouth—

—it's all he can take of this goddamn fight—

—and he breaks into laughter—

—the car careening off the—

—*what the fuck good is this planet anyway?*—

—plunging through underbrush—

—left fender wrenching two young elms—

—and we are shooting backward through scrub and trees down a slope in a dark charge—

—this ripping, scraping, crackling—

—this *whoosh*—

—the precipitous jolt—

—and we—

—we are—

—what are we—

—we are airborne—

—*yes*—

—that's—

—the battleship flipping end over end—

—and Jackson—

—he's learning to fly—

—Ruthie learning to fly—

—me seizing at the, seat gone, scrabbling for hold—

—the thought firing through my mind *no feeling is the last feeling, and then all of a sudden it is*—

—which is when someone turns the sound down on my life—

—I'm living inside a silent movie—

—the night strobing around us—

—the Oldsmobile flipping slower and slower through the—

—relaxing to a halt in midair—

—and, incredibly, starting slowly to flip in the opposite direction—

—up the hill—

—Ruthie dropping back into her seat, screaming in reverse—

—Jackson landing behind the wheel, weightlessness unmade, laughter fleeing—

—the car gushing out of the trees, off the shoulder, regaining the road, the shoulder, the road—

—and my eyes are closed again because of this spectacular night air—

—this realization building in me that we are finally on our way to the farmhouse, just like Ruthie promised—

—I will tuck myself into Lee's bed—

—pull the chain on the lamp—

—except behind my eyelids there's Jackson gliding three yards off the ground, head first, a human projectile, fifty feet in less than a second, fully aware, inquisitive, beguiled, astonished at the tree shooting toward him—

—skull bursting in a black-red spray—

—*we all die at just the right time*—

—*except those of us who don't*—

—that's what Lee's painter friend Paul Jenkins, long white hair, incendiary white beard, will say early next morning—

—he reaching over to pick up the phone in his Paris apartment—

—nothing in mind except the silver sunlight fogging the room—

—Lee, coffee cup in hand, halted in a half turn at the light-flooded double windows—

—unable to make out what's being said, though already knowing—

—love's thermal transfer—

—how fucking DARE you leave me, you fucking bastard—

—even as she takes her place alone in the front pew at the funeral service four days later in the Springs Chapel, having flown back on the first flight—

—refusing to sit with the Pollocks—

—ordering them to the second pew so she can claim sorrow's spotlight—

—Lee's only expression one of relief as the pastor reads an irrelevant passage from Romans 8—

—God never allows pain without a purpose—

—Willem de Kooning leaning toward her as he passes by afterward, whispering *it's over*—

—whispering almost as an afterthought *I'm number one now, sugar—*

—unaware that within a year they'll be sleeping together—

—and with that I land within Ruthie—

—coming to consciousness among the sweetness of mulch and leaves—

—the atrocity in my lower torso so shattering I'm convinced my spine is broken—

—able to rotate my head only enough to puke—

—the me of us delicately reaching up to check my face—

—determine how much of it is still intact—

—because I can no longer see—

—blood filling my eyes—

—I'm leaking everywhere—

—my nose, my jaw, they're still there—

—I'm still here—

—shot through with the distinct impression I may still exist—

—her arms, my arms, our hands—

—I can't move—

—the awareness reaching me that *here* is a densely wooded area, an incline, a massive tree—

—here an exquisite light illuminating the scene through a cloud of dust—

—from the car, its headlights, resting on its side, windshield smashed, passenger door swung wide, limp like a broken steel wing—

—time returning in increments in the form of the Oldsmobile's jammed horn, a siren up on the road—

—several years later a pair of heavy brown leather boots in front of my face—

—this man's voice asking *what's your name, miss?*—

—and me *where's Jackson*—

—and he *who's Jackson?*—

—and in a fluster the blanket, the stretcher, people running in from all—

—no, that's not it—

—they're not here yet—

—it's just this little girl kneeling beside me dressed in a pink bunny suit, hands curled paw-ish to her chest, asking *do you believe in god, lady?*—

—*of course I do, yes*—

—*well*, the little girl saying, *you can stop now*—

—she pointing one of her paw-hands in the direction of the overturned car—

—and the us of me following, rotating her head, ours—

—squinting to make out through grainy haze, in that breath recognizing what's left of the what I was lying at queer angles beneath the inflexibility of the world—

III

Only the living may be dead.

—Heraclitus

THE FUTURE IS ALWAYS YESTERDAY

Eddie Metzger spent the next two months unable to tell where his delusions ended and his hospital room began.

For a while he sat with his parents on the rooftop of the motel they stayed in for five days in St. George, Utah, to watch the nuclear burst one hundred and fifty miles away in Nevada—the bluewhite flash overrunning the cornflower dawn, the radioactive dust sifting down on the sidewalks, automobile hoods, sticking in Eddie's hair like otherworldly snowflakes as he played hide and seek with his bully sister of the gold goat eyes who searched him out for the sole purpose of stealing his candy and laughing at his pipsqueak fury.

His father who for reasons never clearly spelled out to Eddie didn't accompany the family back to New York (his name ever since forbidden), used to call him Prob and his sister Ob, the former short for Problem, the latter for Obnoxious.

The nurses were gray dreams flickering in his brain. Their voices dissolved into his fretful mother's worrying at the ceiling of their Washington Heights apartment as she cut slices off the boiled chicken to place beside the chunk of iceberg lettuce oozing with Russian dressing on his plate.

We're going to die broke, she said as she sliced. Enjoy your food.

For a while Eddie believed he might be listening to a television show. He believed he might be hearing a news anchor report that first contact had been made, though it was impossible to tell for sure whether the transmissions were message or peculiarity, signal or noise.

Eddie couldn't figure out if the orderlies wrapped him like a mummy in his sheets and wheeled him on a cot to the x-ray room and laid him on a cold steel table under blinding institutional lights once, or over and over again.

Leave me alone, he told them from inside the drugs.

Working, their faces metamorphosed into Jackson's face.

Four Jacksons surrounding his pain.

One by one they kissed their forefingers and touched them tenderly to Eddie's lips in a ritual Eddie couldn't parse, whispering: *We're dead. Ruthie's dead. You're dead. You can go home now.*

GHOST MAPPING

He woke to the sound of an old woman gurgling on the other side of the privacy curtain, the reek of her metallic shit riddling the sunny room.

The dream nurses rushed in.

Through a gap in the curtain Eddie saw the woman flat on her back, sheets tucked to chin, eyes wide in fright, mouth open in amazement at what was occurring to her.

You don't exist, Eddie called to her. Hello? Hello? You over there, I'm hallucinating you.

Death broke open sometime past midnight.

The old woman had been quiet and Eddie was somewhere far inside a painkiller trance, this little boy alone in his mother's bedroom.

She was somewhere else with her cousins for the evening. Eddie hadn't switched on the light when he entered because he knew where everything was. He squatted to pick up his red ball that had rolled in by accident and a hand gloved in bruised, rimpled skin lurched from the blackness and grabbed his wrist in a terminal grip.

Seven versions of the old woman stepped from the closet and walked past the one holding him.

The front door of the apartment unlocked and relocked seven times.

Eddie flinched awake and behind the privacy curtain the old woman was saying through her gurgles *LET! ME! OUT!* and next a priest was speaking Latin, waving a golden chalice, sprinkling holy water across her remainder.

SEASON OF MIRACLES

He woke to a doctor speaking in measured, clinical tones, as if Eddie were somehow capable of processing the inbound information about his broken pelvis, concussion, the months of recuperation that lay ahead, how Ruthie had gone instantly, Jackson instantly, too, the way luck works—that you never know if it's good luck or bad until it doesn't matter anymore.

It's a miracle you survived, the nurse with a small, stiff, pointy-winged white bird pinned to her bobbed black hair told Eddie with pushy cheerfulness.

No, said the doctor, it isn't.

SURVIVAL AS BIRDSONG

Eddie couldn't tell where he was. Piece by piece the scene gathered around him. His name wasn't Eddie now, but Eddy, and Eddy was home, that's where he was, back in the city, limping along the sidewalk outside his scruffy fifth-floor walkup in the East Village near Cooper Square, afflictions still fierce, especially at night, even if shedding off him a little more each day.

Given the shrill sunlight, Eddy guessed it was early afternoon.

Late March, the earth coming back to its senses amid brisk damp gusts.

Cutting up Stuyvesant past the weatherworn brick fronts, the scaly wrought-iron railing, the gated stoops leading to heavy black doors, past the garbage strewn across the sidewalk and banked against the chicken-fat-yellow Pontiac parked along the curb, past a babbling homeless woman with long hair the color of dead lust frizzing out from beneath an orange and black New York Mets baseball cap, knees to chest on a crushed box, obsessively fingering the sidewalk beside her as if blind and in search of a dropped quarter, Eddy found himself recalling how a friend had tried to retrieve Eddy's beat-up suitcase from Jackson's farmhouse three days after the accident, only to come upon his clothes scattered across the front yard where Lee had thrown them out the second-story window.

Later he heard she had also destroyed all the photographs of them taken during their six months together.
Jackson and Eddy had existed.
Jackson and Eddy hadn't existed.
There was no evidence one way or the other except somewhere inside him, which he could sometimes pinpoint and sometimes not.

Limping, Eddy recalled what scientists say about why birds sing just before sunup. It's a way to tell their friends they've made it through another night.

I'm here, I'm here, I'm here, their song says, *so fuck you for another day.*

SIGNAL & NOISE

That's how it started: reports accruing around the homeless.

As if one day they had all tuned into the same broadcast, commenced speaking in delirious synchronized rambles: same rhythms, same vocabulary, same sudden manias.

This preoccupation with movement.

This need to touch everything in sight.

Occasionally some began to bleed from the ears.

Some could no longer keep anything down.

Splashes of bloody vomit spattered the pavement everywhere south of Union Square.

They spoke of how the sun shines from their brains, of heat abstractions and television teeth.

TRAVEL AS ANTI-TELEOLOGAL ACTIVITY

Thirty-five years later, theorists Catherine Malabou and Jacques Derrida decided to collaborate on a work called *Counterpath*, an evolving contemplation by the former punctuated by postcards from the latter mailed to her from cities across the globe as disparate as Istanbul, Athens, and Laguna Beach.

The oddly convivial tone Derrida strikes suggests Malabou and he are on a kind of vacation (a word derived from the Proto-Indo-

European root for *to abandon, leave empty, leave ineffective*), that he has taken an extended holiday from—has vacated—his customary mode of writing and thinking.

The couple travels with each other (in the sense that in the fourteenth century *travel* rhymed in meaning with *travail: to toil, labor, suffer, give birth*, all coming from the Latin word for an instrument of torture: *tripalium*) by not traveling with each other—even as they travel with each other.

Malabou argues Derrida's larger project may not initially seem to resemble a travelogue, and yet it is rife with appeals to and mentions of location, cartography, geography, remoteness, estrangement—so much so that Derrida's oeuvre, which is to say Derrida's life, the daydream house that Jacques unbuilt, charts a kind of contra-odyssey through normative sense-making, normative modes of being-in-the-world, that is continuously and acutely haunted by notions of distance, which ultimately means haunted by notions of mortality—in other words, by Derrida's defining compulsion: inexorable exile.

TRAVEL AS CONTAGION

The CDC speculated a psychiatric disorder had begun seeping through the population.

Then the investigators weren't so sure.

Tests found nothing out of the ordinary about the symptomatic: malnutrition, bronchitis, skin infections, information sickness, routine instances of tuberculosis and HIV—everything one would expect, but nothing more.

Odder still, the contagion seemed to appear throughout an entire sub-community, last from a few hours to a few weeks, and disappear again, only to recur later without warning.

JACKIE/JACQUES

All said and done, this man born in French colonial Algeria to Sephardic Jewish parents (minus, according to him, their Jewishness) under a name he later refused—*Jackie*, for the American child actor and comedian Jackie Coogan, who began his career in Charlie Chaplin's *The Kid* as The Tramp's foundling and sidekick, and renewed it much later as Uncle Fester, the hairless teratoid in *The Addams Family* whose body could mysteriously generate enough electricity to spark a lightbulb— has never written about anything else, especially when he seems to have been writing about anything else.

For Derrida, it's all travel, travail, playful and painful both, all the way down, in some cases through space, in some through time, in all through mind, which is to say with and through flesh born and borne a year after his brother's—Paul's—expired before it had reached its third month, leading Derrida to suspect Jackie/Jacques served as a replacement for someone more substantial, yet ever hidden, a supplement to something stingingly present in its absence, some endless deferral of Derrida.

Like all theory, his anti-teleological activity is less about itself, then, than about something else elsewhere: a persistent form of spectral autofiction.

There is always something else to say.

We always mean more than we mean to mean.

Let us call this Derrida's chaos drawer, his drawer of hope and shame.

THE FAILURE TO LEVITATE

The same syndrome started turning up in Philadelphia, Chicago, Miami, and L.A.; smaller cities and towns throughout Kentucky,

Kansas, South Dakota, and Nevada.

That's when the psycholinguists got involved.

DRIFT, ARRIVAL, CATASTROPHE

By then Eddy was sixty and shocked by that barbed-wire fact. He had imagined one life and lived another. Early on, he used to think things would improve, yet all they did was change. He departed the beauty salon for a position as secretary at a gallery in Soho that went under in the late eighties. Working there, he wrote a memoir about his months with Jackson called *Love Affair* in which he tried to keep his boyfriend alive as long as he could, only it didn't work. All he could do was watch Jackson die time after time.

That's when Eddy realized he wanted to be a writer, the variety of person whose aim it was to wake people amid their dreaming, offer them methods to empathize with other human beings unlike them. Only it turned out no one wanted to publish the result. Editors said it read like an overblown, self-important romance novel authored by a middle schooler.

Besides, nobody much cared about Jackson any longer.

Jackson had stopped being one of the most revolutionary post-war artists and commenced being a toxic lout just as well disregarded. People felt a person could be one or the other, but never both, and so Eddy's boyfriend slowly faded from cultural memory.

After *Love Affair's* thirtieth rejection, Eddy fell into a job as a cashier at Walgreens. For a while after that he incinerated biohazard waste in a hospital sub-basement. Then he took up as a home-care provider and moved from his scruffy fifth-floor walkup in the East Village near Cooper Square to a scruffier, shadow-filled sixth-floor walkup in Brownsville across the Brooklyn Bridge.

There were moments he wanted to put his arm around his little-boy self and tell him it was all going to be okay, everything would work out in the end, but he knew he'd be lying. Never in the course of history had a person seen what was coming at them. He reflected upon why this was, and one day the answer buoyed up like a life preserver: his mother had never taught him how to grow old.

Nobody had.

People taught you how to do calculus and understand chemical bonds. They taught you how it was essential to get a job and pay taxes and go shopping for food and do your laundry. Yet nobody taught you what locked-up joints, stubborn neck aches, ebbing eyesight, growing forgetfulness, inescapable clumsiness, and uninterrupted defeat felt like. They didn't tell you your skin would itch a little more each year you lasted, no matter what you did, or about what Philip Roth had appreciated a long time ago: that old age isn't a battle; it's a massacre.

Old age isn't about wisdom.

It's about burning planes dropping out of the sky.

The younger version of himself whom Eddy wanted to put his arms around—the one who adored the smell of whiskey on Jackson's breath, the taste of it on his lips, the way Jackson backed into him at night, fetal, snoring steadily, some Mastiff dreaming anxious dog dreams, the one who wanted to catch a little of Jackson's masculinity—believed intuitively old age was an infection destined to sicken others, never him.

He knew it wasn't true, except that didn't stop him from believing it was, just like everyone else.

ACTIVE ALERTS

Eddy believed in severe weather events the way others believed in god or sexually transmitted diseases—that they infected you, and, once inside, you were stuck with them forever. You could never make it to the other end of the heavy winds, hail, dust storms, floods. You would never be able to remember how you managed to survive them because in the end you wouldn't manage to survive them. That's what severe weather events were all about. They made you a different person, then a different person.

You wouldn't find them.

They would find you.

And once they did, all you could do was hold on tight and wait for the blackout.

THE INFINITE CANON

The psycholinguists unearthed something surprising when they analyzed the data: the rambles of the ailing shared not only the same rhythms and vocabulary, but also very nearly the same sequencing. In other words, the rambles didn't appear to be rambles. Not in any strict sense. Over a long enough period, the pattern began to repeat, no matter who the speaker.

The infected seemed to be producing something akin to a musical round, an infinite canon, where a number of voices sing exactly the same melody, except with each launching at a distinct interval to weave in with the others.

WHAT TO SAY TO EVERYBODY, EVERYWHERE

One afternoon Eddy opened his eyes to learn he was giving a huge floppy elderly man from Zurich named Stefan a lymphatic massage for his swollen knees in Stefan's Prospect Heights apartment.

This, it struck Eddy, was where his whole life had been going: this minute, this place, this recurrent nothing.

Why?

Stefan sat with his red kimono flapped open to an extent greater than that which made Eddy completely comfortable. Stefan's corpulent legs splayed across his washed-out maroon recliner piquant with dried bodily fluids, salsa sauce, and passed gas. Out of nowhere, eyes closed, he announced to the ceiling: *I'm an old queen. I don't want to be an old queen anymore. I just want to get on the ride.*

At first Eddy thought Stefan was speaking about himself.

Then he realized Stefan was speaking about Eddy, too.

He was speaking about everybody, everywhere.

TRAVEL AS WINTER DOUBT

A thousand years before Stefan uttered those words, Eddy's name wasn't Eddy.

It was Eádweard and Eádweard was a twenty-three-year-old thrall on a Viking longboat.

Of this Eddy was convinced.

How?

He had no idea.

The band whom Eádweard accompanied had recently arrived in North America, making up one in a long necklace of colonizers that stretched back to the Paleolithic hunter-gatherers who fourteen thousand years before had entered the continent from the North Asian Mammoth steppe via the Beringia land bridge and spread rapidly in a pandemic of large, rounded braincases.

Eádweard assisted the band to build a settlement in an area about fifteen hundred miles northwest of Brownsville now known as L'Anse aux Meadows. At the time the land was thick with forests convenient for boat and house construction and hunting caribou, wolf, fox, bear, lynx, birds, fish, seal, whale, and walrus. The settlement covered fourteen acres and contained eight structures fabricated with sod over wood frame. The largest measured one hundred by fifty feet and consisted of several rooms. The lower-rank crew and thralls like Eádweard lived in the smaller ones encircling it. The colony supported one hundred and twenty people and functioned as a base camp from which to launch explorations south.

Over the years the winters turned harsher. Game migrated away as deep snow and sheets of ice crept into the region. That warp in climate, together with mounting hostile relations with the Skræling and the death of the chieftain at the hands of the sweating sickness, persuaded the settlers it was time to pull out.

So they packed up, taking what they could and leaving the rest behind in the event they decided to return, which they never did.

An hour after the chieftain succumbed, his son appeared in the doorway of the main lodge, asking for volunteers to accompany the great warrior-explorer on his voyage to the realm of the dead.

Without hesitation, Eádweard came forward.

This wasn't because Eádweard was especially devoted to his master, though he would be the first to admit he both admired and dreaded the man.

Perhaps that's what *devotion* really meant.

Rather, it was that he had already become depleted inhabiting the foul body swaddled around him. He couldn't fathom what it would be like to endure another five or six years in it until the thing gave up on its own in a whirlwind of breakdowns.

As the sun oranged out spectacularly through the branches netted above them, Eádweard came to understand that you barely feel a sword greeting the bones in your neck.

First a flash, then you are over.

On his knees, hands tied behind his back, Eádweard listened to his executioner take a deep breath above him in preparation for the lethal blow and underwent ninety-four percent of one last thought: *Everybody is already as good as dead. It's just that some take longer to die than—*

DISPATCHES FROM THE DRIFT

I have but one language, Derrida writing in *Monolingualism,* which Malabou quotes in *Counterpath, yet that language is not mine. I feel lost outside French. The other languages which, more or less clumsily, I read, decode, or sometimes speak, are languages I shall never inhabit.*

THE GREAT SILENCE

The CDC alerted the military, which in turn alerted SETI, whose founding idea tracked back to the same year Jackson Pollock's convertible Oldsmobile 88 took flight. That was when the Italian physicist Enrico Fermi asked the world a seemingly straightforward question that proved the opposite: *If technologically advanced civilizations are common in the universe, where is everybody?* Until the current eruption of patterned incoherence, the answer seemed to come down to a symmetrical six. Either the initial assumption is simply incorrect, and technologically advanced life is much rarer than we think. Or our current observations are still incomplete. Or our search methodologies are flawed and we're not hunting for the correct indicators. Or extraterrestrial civilizations already know us well enough not to have any desire to strike up a conversation. Or they have nothing to tell us that could save us. Or the nature of intelligent life, once created, is to destroy itself so quickly that it almost never has a chance to gain the capacity to wave to the universe before going up in smoke, fire, famine, war, and plague.

TRAVEL AS AGING

One day when sixty-seven years old Edda blinked and was seventy-two. Her hearing was dull, her feet whole hurt. She sat at her kitchen table one sunshiny autumn afternoon, sipping coffee and recalling how a friend had tried to retrieve her beat-up suitcase from Jackson's farmhouse three days after the accident, only to come upon her clothes scattered across the front yard where Lee had thrown them out the second-story window.

Later Edda heard Lee had also destroyed all the photographs of Jackson and her taken during their six months together.

Jackson and Edda had existed.

Jackson and Edda hadn't existed.

There was no evidence one way or the other except somewhere inside her, which she could detect less and less, like a bouncing red rubber ball giving up its energy. Jackson and she had been new a very long time ago in another place, where they had constituted another arrangement of cells, which is to say another arrangement of time.

Edda afraid to venture out after dark because the neighborhood wasn't safe for a woman her age.

Edda baffled that her paychecks didn't stretch as far as they used to, even though once a month she sat down at her kitchen table and scrupulously tried to finagle the math in a way that might alter the conspicuous.

At this rate, it inched up on her, she would have to work to the far shore of her seventies merely to keep scraping by.

When she was younger, Edda had unconsciously assured herself inflation would at some point taper off, that what she paid for rent would be what she would always pay. By the time she came to appreciate her willful miscalculation, she had become her mother. Restaurants existed in a dimension she could rarely reach. Movies. Concerts. Journeying to a gallery in the city existed on the same whimsical plane as airballooning in Mozambique.

She burst awake at night agitated, shot through with apprehension, unable to see how it would all turn out.

How had she ever come to believe anyone could design their own future?

That the idea of *later* could somehow embody hope?

Lying there on her back, she stared up at the ceiling, heart hamstering on its grief wheel, little by little picking out the anomalies above her that looked vaguely like black birds.

Crows?

Cowbirds?

Great-tailed grackles?

TRAVEL AS READING

Edda used to have a few good friends who made up the family that was more family than her own had ever been, but most could no longer afford to live in Brooklyn and had moved away years ago. She watched those that remained tumble deeper and deeper into themselves, their own airtight fixations and fussy self-absorptions, like human-sized stars undergoing gravitational collapse.

Several died, and several more, and sometimes it took months before Edda caught up with the news.

It was like when she was in her late twenties and early thirties, and all her friends started popping out babies around her in a frenzied attempt to overpopulate the planet, only now it was death.

Everyone prattled on about it when all Edda wanted to do was anything else, which is when she remembered how her father used to read to her on Sunday afternoons in Berlin after their excursion to the Tiergarten. She would cuddle against his chest before naps and lose herself as much in the deep cadences of his voice and warm nutmeg scent of his body as in the worlds he brought to flower in her. She never wanted him to finish a fairytale. Every time he did, Edda felt a little like she had lost a best friend.

That's why she ended up reading so many books in school.

Once you get some language under your skin, what's to become of you?

It was like her father had always told her: *The more you read, the more you travel. This is why god created so many rainy days.*

Sitting over her coffee at the kitchen table, Edda decided she would take up the practice again. She liked the notion of other minds thinking through her, other hearts suffusing her own. Every day she would host a party of interesting people inside herself.

The only question was where to begin.

After some deliberation, she chose *The Odyssey* because, she decided, she wanted to begin at the beginning.

She felt that's where all the wise why's would most likely live.

That evening she took a seat on her living room couch, glass of inexpensive red wine on her side table, tucked a light blanket around her, slipped into place her heavy black plastic drugstore reading glasses, opened the Robert Fagles translation (which she couldn't remember purchasing, yet which was waiting for her on her modest bookshelf when she checked), and was instantly startled by what she unwrapped in its pages.

All her life she had been under the impression *The Odyssey* was about getting home, no matter what, that that was the only thing Odysseus wanted to do: help win the Trojan War, demonstrate his might (it takes a pillage, she thought), then make his way back to Penelope on Ithaca.

Except that wasn't it.

That wasn't it at all.

The book turned out to be about the exact opposite.

That fight to get Helen back from the Trojans lasts a full decade, only to be followed by Odysseus failing to reach Ithaca for another after that, over which time his crew is killed off and he himself reduced to an impoverished nomad, someone who has fallen so far off the radar that no one—including himself—knows where or who he is anymore.

He thereby becomes the embodiment of his name: the giver and receiver of trouble, the king of pain.

Eventually he washes up on the coast of his own country—except he can't recognize anything about it. That is, even when he returns to Ithaca he doesn't return to Ithaca. Rowdy suitors have swarmed the place, his wife assumes he's dead, and the only being who can identify him turns out to be his faithful, hoary, flea-ridden dog, Argos, who takes one look at him from the pile of cow manure on which he lies, wags his tail, and expires.

Odysseus has been too many bodies, too many places, to call where he is home.

After he slaughters the malfeasants, hangs a dozen household maids for betraying Penelope, you would expect him to settle happily back into his old life.

He doesn't.

He can't.

Instead, he strikes off again to battle the vengeful fathers of the suitors, Athena intervenes, and the epic about return-as-no-return doesn't so much conclude as stumble to a stop.

If you add up how much space *The Odyssey* dedicates to its protagonist on Ithaca, versus how much it dedicates to charting his aimless wandering across the Mediterranean, the book's deep argument comes into focus: the fundamental human condition isn't one of being-at-home at all, but rather one of not-being-at-home.

The only real form of voyage is that into unpredictability and risk, which is another way of saying into living.

This leads Edda to determine, taking a modest sip of inexpensive red wine while listening to her nerves whir and an ambulance ululate on a faraway street, that perhaps she won't resume reading after all.

FABLE OF STILLNESS & FLIGHT

Documents show that from 985 to 1410 Greenland—from which most Viking expeditions to North America launched—was in touch with Europe.

Then came complete silence.

In 1492, the year Columbus set sail with those three small ships from Palos de la Frontera, the Vatican noted no news of *that country at the end of the world* had been received for eight decades.

The bishopric of the colony was offered to a certain priest if he would go and restore Christianity there.

The priest tactfully declined.

The colonizing Vikings and Spaniards were distant descendants of previous colonizers—those early humans who made various unsuccessful forays out of Africa, triumphing at last about 210,000 years ago. Within the next 150,000 years, they—we—became a global species, having interbred with, outwitted, and absorbed the Neanderthals as we moved north. Maybe this says everything we need to know about what *Homo sapiens* are wired to do: move on, settle, become restless, and move on once more, misshapen versions of their pasts lugged over their shoulders like gunny sacks.

Each of our species is to some knotty extent refugee and conqueror both, caught in an unremitting cycle of displacement and replacement— variant of the Runaways, that seventeenth-century Eastern Orthodox sect who held the only way to dodge Satan was to remain in constant motion.

Non-arrival turns out to be our point of departure.

THE GREAT CHATTER

The Great Chatter gradually gave the lie to the symmetrical six. After what appeared to be havoc resolved into what appeared to be order, another set of questions presented itself: by whom, and to what end? There were those analysts who held the opinion that the quasi-patterns revealed, not any accurate text itself, but rather the frailty of reading, how the human brain is designed to seek patterns even when they don't exist in order to create stories that make the universe make sense. Starry constellations. Horoscopes. The falsities we impose on the hodgepodge of history. We are determined to browbeat chaos into cosmos, smoke out comfort. Various religious leaders around the globe were quick to disagree, citing passages in their holy books to argue what we were hearing was nothing less than the voice of god spoken through the meek announcing End Days. While the word-by-word message may not be clear, they said, the intent was achingly so. Penitents flooded the streets, jammed with longing for any Other Side (surely this one couldn't be all there was), even as nonbelievers went about their daily business warring, profiting, polluting, teaching, caring for the sick, loving, cheating, killing, and dying, noting that, whatever this strange phenomenon proved to be in the fullness of time, nothing had actually changed, the world just kept worlding, so one might as well get on with it. Those who espoused crystal-exuberant spiritualisms asserted we were listening to Gaia exhorting us to be more mindful of this rental property we weekended on. The military claimed we were facing a potential threat to national security and advocated internment camps for the afflicted until the situation was sorted out. Anarchists celebrated what they perceived to be the first cracks in the coercive hierarchical order, while democratic socialists berated the rest, asserting we shouldn't be shocked by any of this. After all, we had it coming, this natural consequence of perennial oppression. Conspiracy theories fanned out across social media like locust swarms across wheatfields, alternately blaming the occurrence on a nanobot virus accidentally released from one of Jeff

Bezos's secret laboratories, a government experiment in surveillance gone wrong, and Chinese and/or Deep State research into mind control gone right. Mainstream media covered the event ceaselessly for six weeks, screens everywhere hectic with a welter of clashing points of view. But as it became increasingly evident the correct answer might remain forever out of reach, the event slowly bleached away into the informational background, superseded by what seemed more pressing quotidian concerns from school shootings to the price of milk. A small group of philosophers recalled the Swedish thinker Nick Bostrom's argument from the outset of the century that our sensed reality isn't reality at all, but rather a computer simulation in which we are merely unsuspecting digital players. They postulated we were witnessing the emergence of a bug in the program running our existences, a notion that in certain ways rhymed with various skeptics' contention trailing back at least to that ancient Chinese text, the *Zhuangzi,* housing the Butterfly Dream, wherein the protagonist can no longer decide whether he is dreaming a butterfly, or a butterfly dreaming him. Be that as it may, most scientists came to embrace another point of view entirely: that either The Great Chatter was a missive from an extraterrestrial life form, some perplexing attempt at an intergalactic handshake, or maybe, just maybe, it was that very life form itself come to visit Earth, occupy the planet alongside or inside us, soundwaves comprising that species' bodies.

DISPATCHES FROM THE DRIFT

Derrida postcarding: *The sort of uprooted African I am—born in Algiers in an environment about which it will always be difficult to say whether it was colonizing or colonized.*

TRAVEL AS DROWNING

When Edda was a seven-year-old pink-cheeked blond boy named Edward, his demolished mother and father boarded a British passenger liner in New York with him, his bully sister Ruth, a steamer trunk, and a single suitcase in tow, tan with brown trim.

For some reason this time Edward was English.

For some reason there had been some business failure in Boston on his father's part and now they were returning to Birmingham, where his parents had met and fallen in love nine years ago.

They exchanged fewer than twelve words a day, his mother's face conjuring for Edward a cinched bag, his father's an unending tunnel.

The third-class accommodations were much more comfortable and spacious here than on the ship they had taken from Liverpool to New York when Edward's first memories were collecting in the corners of his brain like dust fluff in the corners of a wardrobe.

Their cabin contained a toilet, a mirror, one pitcher of water, one glass, and two narrow steel-framed bunk beds. Edward shared the top with his father, who after too many beers sometimes cried out from his dreams *the crocodiles are coming!* and lurched awake, unable for the better part of a minute to place himself in time and space, then eased back into his battering nightworld.

Ruth shared the lower bunk with Edward's mother, who slept still and silent as a truncheon hanging on a policeman's belt.

If no one tried to roll over, everything was fine.

They even enjoyed sheltered deck access with seating in a roofed and partially enclosed space between the ladies' room and the smoking chamber. That's where Edward and his sister played hide and seek. He wasn't very good at it, so Ruth always ferreted him out and stole the bronze ha'pennies he gathered, which passengers (who used them as tips for the waiters and bussers) on occasion dropped by accident in their wake as they riched along.

For breakfast, day in and day out, it was the same: lumpy oatmeal porridge and milk.

Edward supposed that's what lukewarm throw-up in a bowl tasted like.

Dinner, though, was Christmas every noon, the fare revolving through roast beef, roast pork, fish, and steak, all with vegetables, rice, and bread.

If this was failure, Edward figured, he would make failure his lifework.

That's what he was thinking one sunshiny Friday in mid-May, just past two o'clock in the afternoon.

The liner was nearing the end of her two-hundred-and-second crossing, and Edward, dressed in his only suit, ready for the fanfare of debarkation, was halfheartedly hiding behind an empty deck chair, dodging Ruth as long as he could before her meanness caught up with him.

Nevertheless, he was unable to stop from peeking out around the striped fabric an inch from his nose at the silver flecks dazzling the water all the way to the horizon. They were even more magical than the alarmingly green rugged cliffs of Ireland's south coast that a little while ago had slinked into view through morning fog eighteen kilometers away on the far side of the ship.

Edward had never met such a green greenness before, less color than sound, less sound than celebration.

The nippy breeze smelled like herring, which recalled to Edward the glum truth that he probably wouldn't see another view like this for a very long time, perhaps not until he had his own wife and children.

He liked that sensation.

It made him feel like the woman in that Walter Scott novel. What was her name? Effie. No, Jeanie. Jeanie or Effie. The point was they were sisters who enjoyed their melancholy thoroughly.

If you were melancholy enough, Edward learned from his father, who read to him from Scott every Sunday evening, you got to become a nun.

Edward reckoned becoming a nun might be taking things a bit far.

Even so, every heartbeat these past few weeks had felt gleamingly new, and soon each would feel like last night's cabbage hanging in the air.

Savoring his gloominess, Edward reached up to scratch his cheek and a great thud kicked him back into the wall behind him.

Another one juddered in, chased by a cloud of fire and black smoke billowing up from the hull.

The deck chair he was hiding behind started sneaking toward the railing as if curious to see where the explosion had originated.

It took Edward a second to appreciate he had started sneaking toward the railing, too.

No: he wasn't sneaking; he was sliding.

What had just—

The deck had pitched down.
That's it.
That's—

The ship was all at once listing starboard.

Out the corner of his eye Edward observed the most extraordinary thing: a huge white bird that had once been his sister spread its wide white wings and glided over the railing amid a flock of other white birds, every face a startled white blur.

DISPATCHES FROM THE DRIFT

Derrida postcarding: *About this first trip to Tunis, too much to say.*
Miracles.

THE PHYSICS OF APPARITION

Only then did the noise overtake Edward—the shrieking, the shouts
from the crew to prepare to abandon ship, the word *torpedo* rising
above the rest until overpowered by the earsplitting steam hiss as
the boilers commenced venting to prevent another explosion as the
seawater surged in. Deck furniture and   *who was the*   baby carriages
and parasols and champagne glasses and tea sets   *and the things he*
and trays and this single red rubber ball tumbling   *and the things*
he didn't know   toward the deck's edge and over. He tried   *and the*
things he did   the things Edward   to scrabble to his feet   *how*
she opened her mouth   how Ruth   but was sitting down again.
He tried to scrabble to his feet and   *all the thoughts that must have*
torn through her   and found himself levitating, carried along by the
panicked crowd, unable to touch the toes of his shoes to the planks
below. People were fighting over lifejackets, ripping them out of the
dismayed crew's hands, thrusting each other aside to grab a little more
future. Edward saw   *what must have crossed his   the U-boat captain's*
seeing the second blast   the unexpectedness of   a man's elbow fly up
into a woman's face as she struggled to wedge herself in front of him
and   *absorbing the information   calculating*   and her nose burst
into blood and she   *only one torpedo   how could*   she crumpled
beneath the rush. The lifeboats   *pride   bafflement   interest in the*
physics of the apparition   had swung off the ship, were dangling on
davits maybe two meters from the railing, the crew endeavoring to
hold the throng in check while they tried to secure the crafts, except
his name was   terrified passengers shoved them away, and   *the*

captain's name   Edward could hear   a young woman   *the German embassy's warning*   a young woman in a fancy dress leaped for one, bounced off its side, plummeted bottom up *Schwieger   that was yes   Kapitänleutnant Walther von Schwieger   from Berlin   a noble family   Edward saw them in a holiday photograph*   the water already congested with bird bodies and debris. It was the same for the middle-aged man in a top hat who sought to follow and   *Edward's father shrugging off the notices placed in U.S. newspapers   nobody would ever dare he said   not even the Huns*   and next a heavyset lady   *look at all those people losing their heads Walther thinking as he watched through the periscope*   with a grimly determined face jumped, caught the rim of the lifeboat under her arms, swung back and forth briefly, which allowed   *he thinking coal dust   that's what   it could have been the coal dust or perhaps*   allowed several passengers to grab the vessel and   *perhaps aluminum powder or that yes*   yank it toward the deck. Others clambered aboard, one of the chains let go, and the lifeboat tore loose, plunging bow first into those bobbing below, and surfacing upside down. The ship was   *and Walther only   Edward could feel it as he was carried across the   only thirty years old   Walther thinking how could one fire a second torpedo into this swarm of people trying to save themselves*   the ship was going down quickly. It had only been nine minutes, ten, since the strike   *count them   just six of forty-eight lifeboats afloat   the rest worthless   good god   have they no discipline whatsoever?*   and already   *a country thick with black humor and flat beer*   already the deck skirting the frothing sea. The *Lusitania*'s bow   *eighteen minutes   Schwieger writing that evening in his war diary   eighteen minutes from first to*   had slipped beneath the surface. Powerless to steer himself, Edward saw the railing   *saw Walther Schwieger's death*   racing toward him. He tried to backpaddle, reached out his legs to push off the shoulders of the elderly woman flung into his path, yelling *put me down!* and an instant later   *two years later   his U-boat sunk by a British-laid mine off the coast of the Netherlands   forty-six kills under Walther's   all hands lost   his last thought that*   he was weightless, wings wide and mouth wide and eyes wide like Ruth's as she took flight and once you were in them   *twelve hundred of nineteen hundred passengers becoming birds scattered around him*   the waves mountainous glacial his waterlogged clothes dragging him down Edward tried to kick off his shoes rip his jacket from people screaming struggling to stay alive a few minutes more is all they and he   *remembered the greengreen of the Irish coast*   fought to keep his chin above the horrible taste   *the silver herring flecks*   but   *he can't remember   the mind has fuses*   in one final abominable gesture the liner upending sliding into   *the touch of his mother's lips*   funnels and masts the last to merge with the Celtic Sea and   *the touch of his mother's lips to his forehead as he merged into dreams   her love filling the leaching into his skin like a balm*   and that terrible short awareness of being sucked under by the massive ship's carcass in a great whirlpool *his mother's voice whispering gently   there's always a torpedo on its way for us sweetheart*   sound muffled ocean pressure   *whether we know it whether we don't*   Edward unable to get his bearings panic-thinking *it's always on its way*   thumping into corpses into rubbish suspended beneath the waves wood shards and unused lifejackets and ornate hats and jellyfish dresses and   *crocodiles*   frantic hands pulling at him pulling him down with them   *crocodiles*   trying to ladder over him toward air and light and the parasols splintered tables oars wine bottles gloves lolling ropes and a brown shoe its laces suspended like anemones   *Walther over his shoulder   giving the order to return to sea* lungs aflame eyes searing arms numbing in the arctic cold he unable to orient as up and down turned frenzy and he couldn't wait couldn't not another second one more and the next he became just another thing hanging there hearing his father's voice its deep cadences his warm nutmeg scent reading to him on Sunday evening saying   *we're dead honey   Ruth's dead   you're dead   you can go home now*   and the bluewhite flash overrunning his vision the huge burst the breadth of the sky and this sentence his last shelter all at once gone.

THEORY AS MIGRATION

Another way of putting it: our word *theory* derives from the ancient Greek *theōrós*, meaning *I am sent to consult an oracle*; *I look at, spectate, observe*; and hence, finally, *I contemplate, consider.*

Deep in its mitochondria, then, theory is a practice of displacement and discomfort clothed in the wish for revelation. To listen to it speaking in tongues is to leave home willingly with the understanding you won't ever return and it doesn't matter, that every one of our houses occupies—at best—somebody else's peripheral vision, like a floater, survives as an uninterrupted dispersion that hangs on fiercely to a nostalgia for something that never existed in the first place: itself.

(*Miracle* another way of asking: *Can I please go home now?*)

Every house is built of liquid architecture.

Imagine theory as a perpetual motion machine rather than a mechanism to reach a sound site of being or belief.

It's Polyphemus, Aeolus, and the Laestrygonians all at once.

It's the suitors taking the place apart.

PROPHECY OF THE ACID DARK

And elsewhere: *I am like a child ready for the apocalypse.*

REALITY IS NOT WHAT IT IS

Edda read the news on her laptop every morning at her kitchen table over a bagel and cream cheese with coffee, watched on her TV every evening from bed over a glass of inexpensive red wine, mildly amused by the human obsession with translating what might in the end prove untranslatable, the idea that everything has to have a reason.

For a few weeks she became animated by the hypothesis put forth by a small group of Swiss physicists, who speculated The Great Chatter might not be from another planet at all, but rather from our own future. Many had argued over the years that the proof time travel is impossible is the absence among us of those visiting from tomorrow. Yet the Swiss physicists were quick to point out that, just as the seeming lack of extraterrestrial visitors does not categorically prove they aren't there, aren't here, taking measurements among us, so too the seeming lack of time travelers fails to prove their nonexistence.

Perhaps what we are seeing is the first debarkation of vacationers, immigrants, squatters, or felons from down the temporal highway, disguised for their safety and/or ours, finding it nearly impossible to interact with us through this archaic semiotics we seem incapable of moving beyond.

Perhaps they are trying to say hello, to say help, to say what in god's name are you doing, to say put your hands up and don't try anything funny.

AFTER THE FINAL NO COMES A YES

Each theory is the manifestation of travel in its largest sense—a motility of assorted ideas from one century to another, one brain to another, one corner of a self to another, bustling with countless conscious and unconscious influences, borrowings, contexts, cultures, traditions, and transformations in the same way that that which we once naïvely referred to as The West (as if "The West" were ever something close to a single entity with geographical and conceptual integrity) has always-already been occupied by somatic and cerebral expats, adventurers, sightseers, guides, expansionists, settlers, seekers, saboteurs, and guest workers from that which we once naïvely referred to as The East, even as the opposite is also the always-already case.

Like human beings, theories survive in direct proportion to their capacity to journey through and adapt to terrain and temporality, compose some sermon about a holocaust, some lesson about metastases, some moral about our ceaseless misreading of the world, permanently marked by where they came from, even as they are marked by where they are as well as where they guess they're going, where they aren't as well as where they will never be.

When we say that word *home*, we are immediately trained to think with affectionate devotion of *family*—without recalling that those three syllables spring from the Latin *famulus*, meaning *servant, slave, property*, behind which floats the abstract feminine noun *famulitas: servitude*, an additional acknowledgment, as if we needed one, that language invariably knows more than we do. If we say to a friend *you know how important family should be*, in a sense we are saying *you know how important slavery should be*, a sentence which puts us once more on Derrida's counterpath, where he asks beside you along the way: *What is education?* and answers before we can part our lips: *The death of the parents.*

THE MOST BEAUTIFUL QUESTION

And this: *Whoever said one was born just once?*

THE CONVERSION OF SORROW

It wasn't long before Edda redirected her allegiance toward theories sprouting from the psychotherapists, many of whom read what was transpiring through a lens that suggested The Great Chatter was an expression of our cultural anxiety in the face of where we were, what we had become—our shared unconscious speaking its exhausted dread before the bleak apprehension of waking up every morning only to find itself in the twenty-first century once more.

What we are listening to, they posited, is the racket of collective misery in the wake of our daily necrosis—not so much, Edda considered, smiling to herself as she reached to click off the TV and take the last sip from her glass, a Freudian slip as a Freudian ball gown.

With that she pulled the chain dangling from the lamp on her side table, her room went dark, and, when she awoke next morning, it was Christmas six years later, she was seventy-eight, and her name was Eduard.

THE CONVERSION OF EDDA

Eduard comprehended straightaway he inhabited a scruffy fifth-floor walkup two blocks west and yet identical to the one in which Edda had gone to sleep more than half a decade before.

Shit, he said aloud, staring up into the half-light, startled to hear an unfamiliar voice with pale Bronx coloring issue from him. *Shit, shit, SHIT.*

THIS WASTE OF SKIN

Close your eyes a minute, he thought, lying there, trying to forget himself a little bit longer, and you'll be ninety.

During the night he seemed to have developed a man-paunch like a fleshy deflated beachball. He raised the covers and examined its sadness, the sadness of his ribby barrel chest and skinny legs mottled purple, this waste of skin.

People don't have any luck changing their names, he figured. It's like changing aftershaves. Do it as often as you like. You still stink deep down.

Eduard eased over to the edge of his bed, ached himself upright, made contact with the trampled shag rug below, and pushed off guardedly, conducting himself toward the bathroom. Rain snicked against the frosted windowpane. Twenty years ago, it would have been snow. Now it maybe dusted once a winter. The rest was drizzle and downpour.

While he slept, Eduard's gait had changed into a side-to-side waddle, as if his hips had fallen out of their sockets. His digestive system had gone balky, his back throbbed, and the cramped room he maneuvered through was a grayish blur, eighty percent of its atoms having refused to coalesce in our dimension.

You shuffle through your years, the best Eduard could determine, and at some point you become like alcoholics and teenagers: people just killing time until time gets around to killing them.

Should he call his sister to pass half an hour with formulaic holiday cheer?

He weighed the pros and cons of this notion as he listened to his pee froth beneath him, the concentrated morning stench of it rising.

He should.

Why?

Why not?

That's what you did with sisters.

Wasn't it?

TRAVEL AS HISTORY

Eduard had never gotten along very well with Rhouth. She was four years older and twice as big as he was in a Visigoth way. She wore her blonde bangs too short and a sneer too pronounced and her gold goat eyes said: *Let's get one thing clear—I am silently judging you.*

Once when she was seven and their mother out with friends for the evening, Rhouth had held Eduard down on the bathroom tiles, wedged his jaws open with her Visigoth fingers, and stuck a half-used bar of Ivory soap in his mouth because he had cursed. Except it wasn't because he had cursed. It was because she could. She spent a good long time that evening perched on Eduard's chest, spelling out in some detail what she perceived to be his shortcomings.

That's who she had been and that's who she more or less remained—smug, smart, strong-willed, loud, never mistaken, always precarious, in some nook of herself petrified she had flunked life and someday somebody would notice, although she was also ready to offer her opinion to anyone in any discipline concerning any subject, whether she knew anything about it or not.

Rhouth wanted to save everyone and be saved by everyone. In her mind she was everyone's captain and everyone's patsy.

Was she wretched, clownish, and complicated?

Absolutely.

Did that make it any easier to tiptoe through her temperament?

Absolutely not.

Perhaps, Eduard thought, he was being unjust.

Still, is anyone just when recalling siblings?

Isn't the real emotional work of siblings to bring out the involuntary liar in all of us?

At seventeen Rhouth went away on a scholarship to a classy New England college. Eduard figured he was finally shut of her. Much to his disappointment it snuck up on him that family meant never being shut of some people.

Rhouth became an attorney and went on to marry Jack Collpok, an equally loud, self-important, overweight financial manager with a bald spot atop his head that reminded Eduard of a tonsure and a patchy gray beard that reminded him that most men shouldn't attempt beards.

Rhouth and Jack had two kids.

Whenever touching base with her, Eduard first had to consult his address book to recollect the kids' names, although he remained confident one began with a C and the other a K.

Children struck him as a less hominidal order of hominids, a sub-category in which he had ever been acutely disinterested. They were like

ABSOLUTE AWAY   153

having a pinball machine implanted in your head. Plus Eduard didn't like getting colds and that seemed to be all children had to contribute to society: mutant rhinoviruses. He objected a priori to being born and therefore held it against others who imposed yet more life willy-nilly on earth.

Rhouth and Jack settled into a nice off-white split-level in a leafy neighborhood in north Jersey encircled by malls, parking lots, pizza joints, and excellent schools.

They invited Eduard to their house every Thanksgiving and Christmas.

We feel so privileged to live here, they announced humbly at the dinner table as each person in attendance was perfunctorily made to enumerate what he or she had been especially grateful for that year.

Eduard couldn't hear what they said.

All he could hear was the meaning behind their meaning.

Look at us! it shouted, arms raised over its head. *Look at our incredibly awesome lives!*

When his turn came, Eduard said: I'm grateful for elastic waistbands.

THE PURSUIT OF TOTAL MORTALITY

And this: *Learning to live ought to mean learning to die—to acknowledge, to accept, a total mortality—without positive outcome, or resurrection, or redemption, for oneself or for anyone else. That has been the old philosophical injunction since Plato: to be a philosopher is to learn how to die.*

INNOCENCE, SIN, REDEMPTION, REPEAT

Eduard stayed single, sometimes happily, sometimes not. He never moved out of the city, even though he could barely afford to stay or articulate why he had put himself in the position he had.

He hadn't been sharp enough to get into a shiny college.

He simply didn't have the push or inquisitiveness.

Instead, he fell in love with a famous middle-aged painter who a few months later killed himself.

Eduard tried and failed to write a memoir about their time together. That's when he learned he didn't know the first thing about memoirs. He had tried to read a few, observed how they sought to gain command over that which can't be controlled, but in the end found them boring and predictable: innocence, sin, redemption, repeat.

After that, he more or less decided to let life happen to him, as if that wasn't pretty much what he had been doing all along.

At each visit with Rhouth and Jack, he watched his sister and brother-in-law drink a little more than they had during the last, saw them wade a little deeper into what he came to think of as the vast ocean of suburban stupor.

They had, he grasped after many years, been highjacked by the ordinary.

THE ART OF SUBTRACTION

Three decades or so ago, when the kids whose names almost certainly began with a C and a K moved away, first to fashionable universities and next into the greater world to ignite the fires of their own families, Rhouth developed a signature scotch-pouring technique that involved filling her shot glass and then letting it overflow into the whiskey tumbler below when no one was looking until she had produced a double that to the untrained eye looked like a single.

It wasn't long before she started using those doubles to wash down Xanax, while Jack commenced complementing his own drinks with

Ambien to help him, he claimed (somewhat defensively), sleep.

You know, he answered when asked, *age*.

Eduard remarked from a distance their high-spirited raconteuring going off the rails by degrees, the stories of their trips to various museums and various restaurants in various countries, wobbly in the knees, stumbling into potholes of digression, floundering onto shoulders of free association, thumping into a series of non sequiturs connected partly by chance and partly by Rhouth's adopted conjunction *howsoever* that seemed to allow everything to connect with everything else.

He looked on as his sister dipped an aperitif shrimp into the cocktail sauce in advance of the Thanksgiving turkey and crunched into it, oblivious that its shell had yet to be removed.

On the drive to visit friends for Christmas dinner last year, displeased with the route Jack steered, resentful of having had to live with him so long, she threw open the car door and threatened to dismount.

Eduard sat quietly in the backseat, bracing for impact.

Shortly thereafter he noticed a certain lack of affect steal into Jack, a scarcity of interest, a shortage of spark, a dragging shamble in his step and attention, a barely discernable lean left when he moved that hinted at more than anyone wanted to admit. Jack had been present and pompous and now he was less so every week, sometimes better, sometimes worse, but never precisely himself. He turned malleable. He turned careless. Without thinking, he would stand in a restaurant and tug up his beltless pants to his ribcage as if nobody else were there.

His mouth stayed open, whether he was speaking or not.

Rhouth seethed.

She hardened into a column of feldspar.

Whenever she spoke with Eduard about Jack, she referred to her husband as The Invalid.

She snapped at him through the day, raged at him through the night for having the nerve to become old, become so leakily grotesque, for what that must imply about her, for his mercilessly leaving her, not all at once, not with a single door slam or curt note magneted to the fridge, but in increments, as if he were having an affair with a nebulous entity in a different reality with which he spent more and more furtive time.

It was as if Rhouth had caught a terrible case of her mother.

On Eduard's last visit, she decided they should meet at a small gallery featuring paintings to enhance couches and rugs bought at Ikea. The place was located on the leafy town's main street named after an Indian tribe or Dutch settler. (The word's etymology remained unclear.)

Rhouth thought Eduard would enjoy the artiness and Jack be able to pass another hour on his train to limbo.

Eduard turned up at the corner across from the gallery five or six minutes early. Waiting for the light to change, he saw his sister and brother-in-law come into view a block away on the far side of the street. Rhouth was walking at her usual pace, the one that would lead passersby to assume the important meeting she was supposed to attend had already begun without her. Jack shambled a hundred feet behind, wearing his permanently dumbfounded expression, cell phone pressed to his ear, apparently trying to call his wife to ask her to slow down and wait for him.

Eduard watched as his sister dipped into her purse, plucked out her own cell phone, clicked it off, and slipped it back in, all the while trudging forward with her too-short bangs and furious determination.

Watching, Eduard sensed something inside him shrinking.

Then he sensed it shrinking some more.

And then he sensed it wink out altogether.

ELECTRICAL SYSTEMS AS VOYAGE DEVICES

This year was the first they didn't invite him over for the holidays. Eduard had waited. And in the end he came to appreciate that their silence signified Jack was too far gone, Rhouth far too ashamed, to send up the vestigial social flare.

It was awkward for Eduard to admit, but their remoteness relieved him.

Their situation wasn't his, and he had the end of a life he was busy trying not to live.

Listening to his pee foam beneath him, he resolved to muster the sum of his internal forces and provide Rhouth with a little manufactured enthusiasm.

Why?

Why not?

Ten minutes, twenty, and it would be over, after which he could work out how to unthread the rest of this stupid consensual hallucination of a holiday to his liking.

So in the gray blur of his bedroom Eduard tugged on his washed-out black yoga pants, black T-shirt, and black sweatshirt, his balance during the operation repeatedly disputed by his limbs.

He shuffled into the kitchen, flipped alive the harsh fluorescent light above the sink, and made himself breakfast.

Over his coffee with bagel and cream cheese, he read feel-good holiday stories on his laptop. They infuriated him. The problem was there were no others available, the media intent on keeping revenues robust by shoving everyone into cheerfulness's path. Breakfast was article upon article about triumph over adversity, charity, essential human goodness, mall Santas learning sign language for the deaf kids, drowning dogs plucked from thinly iced-over lakes at the last second.

Sometimes those feel-good stories were accompanied by feel-good photos and/or feel-good videos, which Eduard would put money on were simply recycled versions of the same ones he had endured last year, interchangeable as photos of babies, nails, or gravel.

Outside, the rain intensified.

Inside, the air dampened.

Done, Eduard peed again. Holding it for more than an hour these days had devolved into peril. He returned to the kitchen table, made himself comfortable, took out his phone, checked on the kids' names (which, much to his wonder, turned out to be Olivia and Liam), dialed, and, next thing he knew, he was lying on his back on his vinyl floor patterned with bright yellow daisies set against an unbelievably green backdrop, examining the ceiling from a perspective he had never assumed before.

His inhalations and exhalations were coming fast as bumblebee wings. He had broken out in a theatrical sweat. His back muscles pounded. Sprawled awkwardly to his sides, his arms made Eduard look as if he were attempting horizontal semaphore.

Hello? Rhouth said on the other end of the line.

Some beast grabbed Eduard's heart in its fist and compressed.

Hard.

Eduard's phone lay two feet away on another continent. His jaw clamped shut in marvel before what was transpiring. He couldn't talk if he had wanted to, which was fine, because he didn't especially want to, not now, not like this.

The event was finally here and he didn't want to miss a thing.

He was impressed by how rapidly everything was running at him.

You hear about it all the time, but when you become the narrative epicenter it is extraordinary how experiences feel both like they're befalling you and someone else who only happens to share your name. Eduard had been Eduard less than a minute ago, and now—

Despite that harsh fluorescent light over the sink, the kitchen commenced scattering into quanta.

Eduard looked at himself looking at himself looking.

Hello? his sister said from somewhere in Greenland. Eduard? Is that you? Is everything—

He speculated from within an urgent red fog about the possibility of answering, only the beast grabbing his heart tightened its grip and that thought was supplanted by another.

So this, Eduard Metzger thought, *has been my life. How the fuck about that?*

Hello? Rhouth called from the icefloes. Hello? Hello? *Hello?*

DISPERSAL TRUANCY

And this, too: *If things were simple, word would have gotten around.*

RE•LETHE

People across the planet cautiously acclimated to The Great Chatter, making slow truce with it, giving themselves over to news outlets, politicians, and influencers to oust the unforgiving mysteries with fresh flavors of allure, further visions of beautiful trash.

A British royal diagnosed with late-stage non-Hodgkin's lymphoma went on the talk-show circuit, claiming he had proof Big Pharma had discovered a cancer cure decades ago but had kept it secret for fear of profit loss. His handlers ran algorithms as the metaverse lit up, calculating audience reach, clickthrough, brand awareness, engagement rate, the likes, the loves, the wows, the gentle bells of appreciation.

Delivery drones mutilated unsuspecting pets wanting to play. Neighbors videoed the horrors from their stoops and kitchen windows in listless suburban astonishment.

Reddit. GrimSanta. BoredAssassin.

A young trending female actor accused an old trending male director of sexual improprieties the day before the young trending female actor was herself accused of financial vulgarities by a mantrap male assistant who was accused a month later of drinking dark web tiger blood to enhance his warlock powers by his tweetheart ex-girlfriend-and-sometimes-model who turned out to be in cahoots with a chic bleached-blond billionaire in a plot to lure underage boys to his private island in the Caribbean for parties of a distinctly outré nature.

Everyone in the debauchery chain scrupulously denied the allegations while displaying a faultless balance between simmering outrage and raw vulnerability.

Academics studied how news exists to vanish at carefully computed velocities.

The touchscreens, the light sensors, the replacement appendages.

The disappearing content.

The evergreen content.

The sentiment analysis.

On any given day, about sixty wars continued being waged around the globe about land, resources, ethnic identity, power, and/or drugs, mostly in the Middle East, Northwest and Sub-Saharan Africa, and South Asia, though one would never want to discount Mexico and Eastern Europe. Sometimes civilians were blown apart in their homes, sometimes in markets, sometimes on roadways or in alleys, sometimes at checkpoints or while collecting wood or shitting in rocky fields. Sometimes they were shot, sometimes bayoneted, sometimes turned into pillars of flame, raped to death, beheaded, or, months after the fighting had cooled, unzipped by totaled infrastructure, environment, lack of nourishment, lack of work, abundance of disease.

A prominent heavyset offense archaeologist, whose job it was to comb through social media histories of boy bands with an eye toward unearthing the slenderest hints of body-shaming in their posts, took her own life in a warm lemon-scented bubble bath after a body-shaming campaign against her was initiated by a prominent rival.

The last line of her suicide note, a P.S., read: *Please make sure to add an end date to my Wikipedia page and freeze my Facebook account.*

The fear of missing out.

The fear of being included.

Two and a half months through its journey, the first crewed flight to Mars stopped responding to messages from NASA.

The data screaming in.

The data shrieking in.

Sales of a new pill by Pfizer called Re•Lethe, designed to impede memory, skyrocketed.

THE GREAT SLUR

The next day a new order of strangeness, The Great Slur, broke out in the city. What had happened to Eduard's apartment began happening to others south of Union Square all the way to JFK. A nearly undetectable bluish sparkle enveloped buildings, permeated their concrete and brick exteriors, seeped deep inside. A fine shimmery azure haze sheathed furniture, coated walls and fixtures, overlaid everything from toothbrushes, silverware, and ashtrays to houseplants, shoehorns, and spooked cockroaches.

Before the government could respond, inhabitants in the affected area awoke to the slow comprehension that their apartments had relocated to different floors, or, more disconcerting, between floors like stalled elevators. The streets filled with the sound of police and hook-and-ladder sirens. Some apartments manifested in other complexes entirely, while others subtly reordered—a few unsettling inches added to a bathroom, space at the back of a closet gone missing, the height of a ceiling increasing or decreasing by a centimeter or two, a chapter of a novel on a disheveled bookshelf arising earlier than recalled, the advent of typos, foreign words, unreadable languages.

Intermittently doors went away.

Bystanders reported it was as if another existence were infiltrating this one.

As if the anxious perplexity everyone had been feeling recently surged out of them and into their surroundings.

Wives and husbands took in their partners with barely suppressed suspicion, speculating that they, too, had somehow been contaminated by the shadow life, become other than who they claimed to be.

Now that I know you better, they thought to themselves, sizing each other up, *I know I don't know you at all.*

Five buildings from Queens glittered into being across the East Village, overlapping with those already in place to create elaborate Escheresque configurations in whose impossible hallways tenants became irremediably lost, followed by the search teams in spelunking gear sent in after them.

Katz's Deli on Houston Street blipped out of existence altogether, taking everyone inside with it.

The ninety-three-story Brooklyn Tower snapped into view at twilight, fully intact, in a remote area of the Nevada desert near an old nuclear testing site.

That evening a 747 bound for Heathrow tilted up its nose for takeoff at JFK and vanished along with all but three of its four hundred six passengers, two of whom moments later flickered back into being at separate airport terminals, one at the Suvarnabhumi in Bangkok, one at the Galeão in Rio de Janeiro. The third appeared at sunrise the next day on a seldom-used LAX runway, curled into an embryonic ball, thirty years older, hair white and frowsy, torso bruised, stammering about the bitter taste of sound and how thought ice is the most painful kind of motion there is.

New York declared a state of emergency.

New Jersey. Rhode Island. Connecticut.

The banking industry faltered.

The stock market tumbled.

At twilight, thousands of National Guard troops flooded into

Manhattan, along with military flatbed after military flatbed loaded with blast walls, quarantining the area below Twentieth Street and all the boroughs on the far side of the East River.

Tanks surrounded the Brooklyn Tower. Smartphones in hand, flummoxed onlookers drove in from Los Angeles and Las Vegas, St. George and Ash Springs, to gather at the security perimeter and document the inconceivable. The news crews. The newlyweds. The sun-staring visionaries living in trailers sans air conditioning scattered across the desert calamity.

Attack helicopters circled the skyscraper, a swarm of enormous titanium wasps.

SOUND POEM OF DEFEAT

Another way of putting it: aging is time travel gone awry. It has less to do with grandchildrening or grace than with arteries ossifying muscles waning ligaments locking constipation killing isolation flourishing bones brittling bladder abating brain smudging stairs intimidating stamina softening finances uncertaining showers endangering mutations partying cataracts hazing diabetes menacing new gadgets strong-arming hearing blunting breasts deflating tummy jellying teenagers threatening downtowns threatening viruses threatening bacteria threatening death of a spouse threatening care providers threatening giving up the car keys threatening giving up the house keys threatening dignity retreating gums retracting hurt inflating fashion kidding longevity laughing speed alarming skin rice-papering taste drabbing boredom ballooning wrinkles flocking spinal discs crunching lungs shriveling immune systems wilting sex organs drying sex organs unfirming sex organs retiring sex organs renouncing metabolism dragging nerve signals stuttering change changing evolution hectoring telomeres burning down, burning down, burning down.

It's like a miracle, only not at all.

DISPATCHES FROM THE DRIFT

Postcarding: *Have I told you my mother's maiden name, Safar, when spoken with a certain accent, means* voyage *or* departure *in Arabic?*

THE GREAT FLUCTUATION

Thanatologists took a different tack. They posited The Great Chatter and The Great Slur were intrinsically connected. In fact, they were two sides of the same phenomenon the thanatologists termed The Great Fluctuation.

They submitted what we were hearing were the voices of the dead, the cities' homeless their intermediaries, earbuds made flesh and bone.

What we were seeing was a keyhole through which lay the life hereafter, a brief (on the scale of eternity) bulletin sent to let us know what we can expect following expectation: deafening babble and boundless confusion.

If you believe our lives here and now are treacherous, the dead seemed to be telling us, just you wait.

If you believe the beyond will ultimately provide a sanctuary of stillness and serenity, keep jerking your own chain.

The bulletin behind the bulletin proclaimed: *Enjoy every in-suck of breath. You have fewer left than you think.*

Or conceivably the inverse was true. Conceivably The Great Fluctuation was evidence of the dead's compassion. Maybe they were actually trying to calm us, affirm that everything was going to be— after a fashion, give or take, roughly speaking—all right, fine, good enough, by showing us that what comes next won't be as bad as our faiths have viciously taught us.

Death wasn't nothing, granted, no snapped-off light switch, no ebbed battery, but it wasn't hell either, wasn't Job on a bad day, white tunnels, reincarnation, spirit worlds, nine realms or seven, unconsciousness, family reunion, judgment cataclysm, gray in-between, a summer meadow bustling with furry Norsemen, or bright balls of divine light.

What awaited us was no more—and certainly no less—than an unending low-grade mayhem, not unlike this life, only louder.

Or perhaps it was that the departed weren't even aware of us, couldn't see us, had no sense of our presence, couldn't have cared less, had simply begun spilling out of their elsewhere because it had become so crowded over the millennia, that what we were hearing was them calling out in alarm at the disruption to their non-lives, asking what had happened, where they were, begging to be let back in like cats on a snowy night.

By the time those thanatologists spoke up, however, no one was paying much notice anymore. Too many conjectures had been put forth only to be contradicted, bickered about, pushed aside.

The Age of Interpreters had come and gone.

All people wanted nowadays was to eat their breakfast in peace, then take the dog for a walk. All they wanted was a not-heinous McJob with benefits, including dental and vision. If they had a few minutes to nap, watch a flea-brained movie, scroll through a dozen social media sites, type a couple dozen texts while lamenting how many texts they had to type, and share a beer around a chiminea with acquaintances they could pretend were more than acquaintances in a backyard they could pretend was more than drab, they were content.

Who cared about what was going on Out There when everything worked plenty well In Here?

Who genuinely cared about havoc when it wasn't yours?

DESPERATION NATION

There came the talk of clarity. Of healing. Of breath and balance and opening hearts.

All at once everything was personal.

All at once everything was public.

All at once everything was Zoloft, Paxil, Wellbutrin, Ozempic, and radical love.

Because the only thing big questions ever led to were big agitations. Thought has always been the greatest trauma trigger of all. Whereas the touch of somebody's lips on your right shoulder, the sensation of somebody's arms tightening around you as they draw you in close, the numb mind in the middle of morning meditation pretending it's alert: those are the only solutions that matter—those and perhaps the latest video console, a good Sunday football game, a toke of high-grade weed, some flyfishing in a mountain stream a couple yards down from someone else flyfishing in the same mountain stream (nothing like the tug of a trout on the line; the crack of its skull against stone; the caveman thrill of it), a few happy hours a week at the your local taproom, chilling, putting up your feet, letting down your hair, before passing a smeary evening boozing and gambling at your nearest seedy casino.

If there were more to life, people said, one skeptical eyebrow arched, they'd sure like to see it.

There came the talk of classical guitar lessons. Yoga studios. Adult education classes.

The talk of intention and surrender.

Of high-end hazmat suits, the flexitarian diet, Self-Isolation Advocacy.

The book clubs.

The microbreweries.

The celebrity doppelgängers, the trend forecasters.

Squat challenges and moon phases.

Everyone is precious.

Everyone is dangerous.

Unicorns vomiting rainbows and the Shellshock Massage developed to follow that dim squander called your dayshift.

That's how the movement Joy Pride™ burgeoned. Its motto, printed in plain black Baskerville on white T-shirts, sweatshirts, and baseball caps: *I missed the part where that's my problem.*

The healthy salads with kale, flaxseed, and dried cranberries preceded by a Klonopin, an Ativan, a BuSpar.

The side of grilled salmon.

Of grilled chicken.

The CBD gummies.

The talk of black carbon aerosol, habitat fragmentation, flavor fatigue.

Of going with the flow. No coincidences. The biome.

The tactical vitamin supplement.

Self-care and TikTok. Jade eggs and vaginas. Celery juice and kombucha.

The Corpse Pose.

Words like *Asiacentric, nomophobic, whatevs.*

The Sky Destroys the Rabbit Pose.

That tingle of superiority sensed in the modest everyday display of kindness and gratitude.

The list of drawbacks to empathy.

The boosted post. The dark post. The hashtag.

The listicle. The lurker. The cost per mille.

Newsjacking and vanity metrics.

Quantcast and coffee enemas.

Oxygen shots and Yelp.

Placenta pills. Penis facials. Eco-friendly menstruation.

The information coming in.

The information going out.

DISPATCHES FROM THE DRIFT

And: *How can one be late to the end of history?*

THE INCORPORATION OF FELICITY

Joy Pride™ went public one month after incorporation, making its founder, that chic bleached-blond billionaire with a propensity for parties with juveniles on his private Caribbean island, resplendently richer. He took to the cable networks in a flowing white robe, part guru, part Mormon Jesus, to offer humble thanks, nondenominational prayers, and special discounts for those who ordered more merchandise within the next fifteen minutes.

TRAVEL AS METEMPSYCHOSIS APPARATUS

When we say we would like to go on holiday, it crossed Edda's mind, a different Edda's mind, startled to have occurred back on her living room couch one damp summer evening, Lattimore translation of *The Odyssey* winged open in her lap, which became his living room couch, his lap, became Ed's, Ed Metzger's, glass of inexpensive red wine in hand—when we say we would like to go on holiday, we are saying we would like to reorganize our identities for a while within a safe ecosystem.

The Great Fluctuation had subtracted the final remnant of Ed's interest in stepping out of his sixth-floor walkup. Not even for the occasional slo-mo afternoon shamble with the help of his walker. Not even for the short trek down to the bodega.

The military vehicles in the streets, their diesel murk, the jabber of the homeless lining the sidewalks, the city's frightened inhabitants

dashing from one block to the next before everything shifted again—
who needed that at his age?

Everybody looked like refugees.

Everybody looked like they were dodging snipers.

Ed ordered in groceries. Sometimes they arrived and every so often
they didn't. Sometimes the boxes contained what he had asked for and
now and then it was something else. He was low on coffee beans and
milk, though he took solace in his ownership of two dozen eggs.

There was Spam.

There was always Spam.

Bouillon cubes, both beef and chicken.

Dried beans and canned tuna, foodstuffs which would outlive the
earth itself.

Sometimes the toilets didn't flush. Once in a while he found his
flashlight in the oven, the book he was reading under the mattress.
Every so often the electricity went out and the internet down. Almost
every day he located a shelf, lock, or drawer where there hadn't been
one the day before.

Cries of dismay issued routinely from the stairwell.

Each morning Ed awoke sure that what lay on the other side of his
front door would constitute a surprise. A big one, a small one. He never
knew which until he peeked through the peephole, if today his door
possessed a peephole. What he did know was that he would uncover a
floorplan other than the one he had left behind the night before.

Inching out of bed had evolved into an act of negotiation,
determination, and senselessness.

What was the point?

The difference between waiting for the day to pass, prone, versus
waiting for it to pass, upright, ruminating on how the preterit turns out
to be the saddest tense in creation, on how getting older was getting

used to losing somebody or something or some ingredient of yourself every few hours, was what, exactly?

Why throw away all that hope he had hoarded in his sleep?

Why let it break into littler and littler pieces before lunch until all that was left was the humid air enfolding him?

Going on holiday, Ed thought, sipping his wine, considering Odysseus, was nearly the exact opposite of travel.

Sure, like travel, we go on holiday to become someone else for a while, ruin the sovereign self. We use movement to change perspective, gain perspective, reexamine our routine lives, turn a bracelet of hours into an exercise in focus and inquisitiveness, reconsider the personality that has accumulated around us, some identity we bought off the rack at Urban Outfitters, at Zara, at J.Crew, rediscover those crannies of us that have been there all along but have been disappeared by everydayness, tucked behind the simulation of that first-person pronoun we wear like a crinkled-edged badge at a Better Business Bureau conference.

Going on holiday is contemplation turbine, energy generator, understanding amplifier, an essential reminder that in the long run it really *isn't* all about us.

Sort of.

Yet, unlike travelers, sightseers expect to be pampered by fancy hotels between rides on hermetically sealed buses with excellent views of the natives.

The fanny packs. The white socks and beige cargo shorts.

The floppy hats and perfect teeth and endless supply of floss.

Sightseers want to be reminded it really *isn't* about us, while it most definitely is, of course it is, dollar after dollar, which is another way of saying fancy hotels function the same way McDonald's do. No matter where they crop up on the planet, their mission is the same: make our surroundings slightly unfamiliar in a very familiar way.

Fancy hotels let us bolt the door against the jumble outside so we can indulge in luxury, special secrecy, a cordoned-off microcosm, a little corner of wonderland replete with snack bar and fluffy robe and maid who barely knows English and cleans up after us for a scintilla above minimum wage.

Sometimes we will smile at her as we pass her cart in the hall.

Sometimes we will act as if we don't notice her, can't pick her out from the wallpaper, to save us both the discomfort at what we know.

If we are lucky, there will be a jetted bathtub.

Premium bedding and a free square of mint chocolate waiting for us on our pillow.

Fancy hotels are by nature a travesty of home that impersonates home, a perversion of the domestic, the embodiment of ontological corruption that resides in an eerie sphere with ridiculous physical laws all their own.

The T-shirts palimpsested with brand loyalty.

The unremitting happiness.

The sun visors worn nowhere else.

The bedazzlement before anything old, ice cubes, and the dearth of ketchup.

According to psychologists specializing in travel theory—and despite the current vogue for producing lucrative clichés about living in the now (Ed grins to himself, mulling over whether we should try harder, rather, to live in the how and why)—the truth seems to be something else entirely: that we spend much if not most of our mental lives dwelling in the future.

That's unsurprisingly how humans are carpentered, because dwelling in the future is an essential survival strategy. Try doing the inverse. Try living in the present or past for ten minutes and you will almost surely hurt yourself, singe yourself, shoot yourself, walk into a door frame, drown yourself, poison yourself, starve yourself, slice yourself, gorge yourself, sugar yourself into a coma, run a stop sign, fall off a balcony, tumble onto the tracks, selfie off a cliff, end yourself early.

The leisure travel industry gets this at a structural level and so emphasizes future-mindedness as a mode of pleasure.

Holidaying means planning, itineraries, expecting interesting things, new-but-not-too-new things, and that gives us something to look forward to. Consequently, we commence consuming our trip long before we embark on it. We imagine ourselves having Petra all to ourselves—as Ed did to celebrate his retirement from the university decades ago—months in advance of boarding that flight at JFK. We picture ourselves lounging outside a Parisian café on the Champs-Élysées, sampling our overpriced cappuccinos—as Ed did to celebrate his college graduation more than half a century ago—weeks ahead of heaving our oversized backpack from the recesses of our closet perfumed with ragged sneakers.

The travel industry coaxes us to enjoy envisioning enjoyment long before we near the stimuli themselves, or, perhaps closer to the point, the real stimuli aren't real at all.

Tourists buy a romance which lasts much longer than the clock-time reality, and it is that which helps them forget about delayed flights, family of baboons snorting in the seats behind them, hysterical turbulence over the Pacific, lost luggage, insipid tour guides, crammed tourist sites, stolen wallets, unanticipated cloudbursts, filmy jetlag, truculent beggars, popped blisters, scam artists intent on ambush in the dash between bus and museum entrance, gangs of adolescent pickpockets scoping, failed credit cards, busted cell phones, food poisoning.

The travel industry knows something we don't: that our brains are hooked up to misremember assiduously because bought romance is configured to absorb genuine recollection.

Narrative's Ur-function, it turns out, is to overwrite the actual.

Tourists possess a profound involuntary recognition that going on holiday incorporates well-defined beginnings and endings.

We relish our anticipation of moderated novelty, assume we have procured a certain small degree of uncertainty, insecurity within secure boundaries, bicycles with existential training wheels. We shell out for just enough instability to make each minute feel uncommon, yet not too uncommon, fresh-breezed, yet not blustery, just enough sensory spice to keep our attention-palate activated even as we remain thousands of miles away from the blight of serious pileup.

Which is the perfect definition, Ed realized as he picked up the paper Odysseus napping in his lap, of reading, this thing he is embarking on this very second—this odd, exclusively mortal act involving flexible tree pulp and black squiggles that effect the transmigration of fear and yearning from one soul to another through the fuzzy tail of comets.

TRAVEL AS FAMILY

Done, Ed peed again. He returned to the kitchen table, took a seat, tugged out his cell phone, checked on Ruthie's kids' names (which, much to his wonder, turned out to be Emma and Noah), and dialed.

He sipped his coffee inside a morning cloud of photons, anticipating.

Once the ringing starts, he knew, there's no escape.

They know who placed the call, what time, who hung up before—

I don't understand anymore, Ruthie was saying out of nowhere.

It was as if they had been talking for hours and she just concluding. Her voice warped across icefloes, overran with static and then cleared.

It used to—, she said. And now this. What is this?

Merry Christmas, sis, said Ed. What are you and Jack up to today?

We're up to Jack is sleeping. That's what we're up to. That's how Jack Jacks lately. Can you point out Slovenia on a map? I can't. I'd hypothesize near Hungary. But then the question becomes: Where is Hungary? It's like that, all the time.

Everything feels obsolete, Ed said. Two minutes ago—prehistory. Three—the primeval fireball. Why go out?

There's enough crap to deal with staying in. Do you know what the checkout guy at the convenience store told me yesterday when I asked him to please use hand sanitizer before touching my products?

I don't.

He told me I was harshing his mellow.

People talk like this?

Unselfconsciously, Ruthie said. He wore metal things instead of eyebrows, which he had shaved off. Imagine the distress of insertion, I thought, standing there, trying to invent a witty rejoinder.

What did you come up with?

I apologized.

You apologized was your witty rejoinder?

What happened to Rhodesia? Bengal?

The GPS is busted. We're coming in hot. How are Emma and Noah doing?

How should I know? Ruthie said. They're doing fine, I'm supposed to say. I'm supposed to list their recent accomplishments and the accomplishments of their children, then feign maternal pride. Then you're supposed to perform supportive delight. They're doing great, I'm supposed to say. They couldn't be better. Which I will make something up if you'd like. I think Emma may have an eating disorder. Either that or she's taken up running.

What from?

Her zombie life as barista at forty-two, if I had to wager a guess. Don't you worry about it all? I do.

I want to lose interest in it all, Ruthie said. That's what I want. What are the chances, do you think?

One in a trillion, Ed said.

My husband, this man I have known and loved and not loved and loved again for however many years—now it's Häagen-Dazs. This is who he is. Ice cream has come to determine his Jackness.

Häagen-Dazs, Ed said.

He looked out his kitchen window at the grungy brick wall ten feet away which hadn't been there a month ago.

Once it was painting, Ruthie said. Once it was time in the studio. Now it's ice cream. He smiles while slurping. If you can call that thing he does a smile. Ice cream and pepperoni pizza. The New York kind with pooling grease that saturates the paper plate beneath until orange and slimy. But mostly Häagen-Dazs. Strawberry and chocolate-chocolate chip. That's what we talk about. The banks coming apart? Climate refugees? Forget it.

The temperatures, Ed said. The aridization. Telehealth. I'm sorry.

Think five years, said Ruthie.

How so?

Don't be sorry. Who can be sorry when you think five years?

It's all our fault.

How?

Fuck if I know. We had occasions, evidently.

Everybody has occasions, Ruthie said. Heart-searing guilt is the new black. Urgently feigned Zen indifference. An emergency irony that implies we had it coming, that announces: *If only you people had listened to me.* New flags, new threats, new deceptions, and it's: Where's my strawberry ice cream? Where's my chocolate-chocolate chip? Chocolate salted fudge truffle, I should mention, is out of the question. Don't even get Jack started about the deficits inherent in sorbet.

This is a problem?

This is a breakfast.

Give it to him. It's the least life can offer by way of atonement.

What was democracy?

The total saturated fat. The rush of sodium through the arteries.

And they say: Be grateful.

That it isn't worse, Ed said. What was privacy? Here, have mine. I'd rather chalk up likes on Facebook. I'd rather be able to buy overpriced items on Amazon while simulating meaningful relationships.

It's everyone's above average.

Botoxed and detoxed.

Everyone's a winner.

Except those who aren't. Super-predators, for instance. As opposed, I assume, to run-of-the-mill predators. The word *impactful.* How are your eyes doing?

Macular degeneration is a breeze, I'm supposed to say. Hangnail annoyance. This is the point in our conversation where I'm supposed to downplay the repercussions of slowly losing my eyesight and lead you to feel pressured to say with a mixture of encouragement and affirmation that I'm built from pure grit. Look at me. I am woman. Hear me stoicize. Which I will make something up if you'd like.

Jesus.

Do you happen to know if Dupuytren's contracture runs in our family?

Why do you ask?

It just occurred to my synapses, she said. They wondered, not me. I couldn't care less. This is the point in our conversation where you're supposed to ask what's in store for Jack and me today. A shuffle around the block? A witless movie on the couch accompanied by clever eyerolls undergirded by a sense of critical sanctimoniousness?

What's in store for you and Jack today?

Häagen-Dazs and autonomous synapses. That's where my lifework has taken me. That and wondering where the alley went I used to look out on from my bathroom window. It was here a week ago. There was a cat. White and bloated. A furry pocketbook with legs. Its owner had dressed it as a French nihilist. Red beret. Red ascot. Black-and-white striped Breton fisherman's shirt. Said owner, a thousand-year-old Asian woman bent into a merciless head-forward posture, had leashed it. The cat craved euthanasia. You could see it in the eyes.

Dirty bombs, Ed said.

Sliding markets, said Ruthie.

The seepages. The investigations. The unknown unknowns.

Help me out here: what's trauma porn?

Don't ask. In Japan you can rent a mother. A father.

One of each has been plenty for one lifetime, thank you very much.

Grisly information's advent as booming industry, Ed said. Big numbers. Batch processing.

Data lakes.

Raw water. White noise machines. Discussions about collective helplessness.

Superfund sites. The next variant after the next variant's variant.

The arsenic dust storms once referred to as the Great Salt Lake.

Don't worry, said Ed. Be happy.

Live, laugh, love.

Have no regrets.

Forgive yourself.

Do no harm.

Let it be.

Let it go.

Just go for it.

Just do it.

Just do the work.

Just get over it.

Just get on with it.

Life is short.

Life is a journey.

Life is a short journey.

It was meant to be.

Shit happens.

You can't take it with you.

Embrace the wonder.

Follow your bliss.

Feed your soul.

Today is a gift.

Tomorrow is an exchange of that gift for one that fits.

You got this, girl.

Crush it.

You're only as strong as the drinks you mix.

Stay grounded.

Stay present.

Balance your chakras.

Balance your meds.

Be yourself.

Be anyone you want.

Don't leave home without it.

Wait, Ed said, staring at the grungy brick wall out his window. I think that's a corporate tagline.

These are all corporate taglines, honey.

I hear you.

I see you.

We believe you.

You are worthy.

Run wild.

Run like your goddamn life depended on it.

Don't dream it. Be it.

Take back the night.

Don't forget the afternoon.

Wield your stun gun like you fucking *mean* it.

. . .

. . .

. . .

. . .

. . .

. . .

...

...

...

...

...

...

...

Well, that was fun, Ruthie said. What do we do now?

...

...

...

...

...

...

You would imagine there should be a way to outthink the difficulties, Ed said, wouldn't you?

I take some small consolation in the knowledge the world may be melting down, said Ruthie, yet we still have punctuation. God bless the Oxford comma. God bless the em dash used with panache. Except—why do you suppose no one speaks about the imminence of nuclear war anymore? I have to confess I feel a certain gentle nostalgia for its terror. The good old days of duck and cover. The shadows on the walls. The turtle in his shell. The cartoon children beneath their cartoon desks. His name was Bert. Why do I have to recall this? Speaking of which, you know what I picked up at the pharmacy Monday?

What?

My first prescription for Re•Lethe.

You and Jack can forget together. It'll be romantic.

Like binge-watching in pill form. I can already feel its first effects, though the label says it doesn't really kick in for two weeks. Plus or minus. I can't wait. By the way, I suggest we give ourselves a different name for each phase of our lives.

Because why?

Because we're never us. Because every day is identity theft.

Because our computers are trying to kill us, Ed said. Because gray goo and insurgents on the crosstown local. Because someone is short-circuiting our power grids on a regular basis. Let's call it North Korea. Let's call it a teen named Dylan sitting in his basement in Hackensack, eating Doritos.

Did you have light last night?

I read by it, Ed said. You would have thought we could have considered vulnerable power grids at an earlier date. How are Noah and Emma hanging in there?

You already asked that.

Oh.

What were you reading?

The Odyssey.

Spare me, Ruthie said. I used to be a respected attorney fighting the good fight against whatever it was I was fighting the good fight against. Soon it will be the Cyclops. Circe. That guy with the prophecy thing.

Tiresias?

How should I know?

You've read *The Odyssey?*

Of course not, Ruthie said. I saw the seven-minute YouTube video. Talk to me of contingency fees. Talk to me of wrongful death and hearsay and medical malpractice.

Jack's approach, Ed said. It's equally obvious and enticing. Give the man his Häagen-Dazs, sis. May every meal be a holiday treat.

What are you saying?

I'm saying it's on me.

You'll pay for it?

I'll endorse a proof of concept.

You're saying give him pleasure and hope. That platitude.

No, no. I'm deploying a different platitude. I'm saying make him comfortable because what's there to lose?

I'm highly dubious of this comfort business. What is comfort? Go ahead, Ed, define the word in such a way that any two people would agree on its meaning across time and space.

I'm just saying—what am I just saying? I'm just saying—

...

...

...

...

...

...

Hello? Ruthie's voice said from somewhere inside Kazakhstan.
Can you hear me?

Hello? she said. Hello?

I'm right here, Ruthie. Ruthie? Here I am. What if I just— Can
you hear me now?

Hello? Ruthie said. Hello? Hello? *Hello?*

THIS FUTILITY OF CONNECTIVE TISSUE

Ed hung up and lay down his phone on the kitchen table until it
fainted.

He revived it and redialed.

The voice on the other end wasn't Ruthie's.

It belonged instead to someone with an Oxbridge accent explaining
in the register of a BBC documentary: *Long after they had been forgotten,
the nanotechnologists came forth with their account.*

Science on earth, they said, is barely five hundred years old. In that
brief time, we have learned how to read DNA, understand evolution
and radioactivity, eradicate once-common diseases like tuberculosis
and polio, leave earth for another planet, undertake nascent quantum
teleportation, and program machines to process incomprehensible
amounts of data at unbelievable speeds.

Now picture an inhabitable planet (astronomers calculate there
are as many as three hundred million in the Milky Way alone, which

is to suggest we're not talking science fiction so much as the laws of probability) on which science has been extant much, much longer. Around a star older than the sun, life could have initiated a billion years earlier than it did here. Assuming that planet's civilization somehow dodged the bullet of its own murderous self, science would have had millions of years to advance.

Put differently, residents of that planet would have had more than enough time to transcend the faulty organic mess, the meat bags, from which they arose, and emerge as inorganic intelligence. It stands to reason such an intelligence would become smarter at an exponential rate, creating more efficient versions of itself on a timescale inconceivably swifter than the sluggish zoological one Darwin described.

That species would within several hundred thousand years likely launch an exploratory nanotech diaspora across the galaxy to strike up a conversation with whomever else might be out there. Unencumbered by flesh, bone, blood, or whatever else might constitute the rest, that diaspora could continue its mission until, in about a billion years, Andromeda crashes into us, the whole eventually clumping into an amorphous amalgam whose energy the nano-intelligence would by then be able to harness. All the atoms once contained in the stars would be transformed into a single inorganic organism of galactic size and awareness.

That instant would mark the culmination of the long-term trend for living systems: the unremitting increase in complexity.

What we might be watching around us is a relatively early stage of this project: an immense swarm of microscopic probes arriving on earth to integrate with the biological bodies of the dispossessed, the mineral corpus of the city itself.

What, precisely, would the goal be of such an enterprise?

How could we rachet up enough hubris for us to entertain the possibility that such a civilization would have even the slightest interest in us?

That, the speculators concluded, would be like asking a flatworm to explain through differential equations the experiment of which it is part.

DURATION AS BOTCH

Unless, that Oxbridge voice went on, the universe and everything in it was created a fraction of a second before I spoke this sentence, the one you're listening to, this sentence composed of thirty-four words, now thirty-seven, thirty-eight. *There is no logical impossibility in the hypothesis*, Bertrand Russell acknowledged in *The Analysis of Mind* back in 1921, *that the world sprang into existence five minutes ago, exactly as it then was, with a population that "remembered" a wholly unreal past.* Almost in mid-thought, Russell veers away from this assertion and moves on to other topics because, he maintained, the idea struck him as an uninteresting one to consider for any length. Really? Does interest have anything to do with the thorny real? And does a declaration of disinterest accomplish something other than underscoring Russell's bottled-up anxiety before the idea that philosophy can't outmaneuver foundational uncertainty? That his entire intellectual venture is built on shifting sands he doesn't want to acknowledge, let alone examine too closely, for doing so might bring down the whole daedalean edifice? As we construct each of our arguments, we run into despots, siblings, saints, liars, letches, lotus-eaters, masochists, mothers, murderers, poltergeists, prudes, and pogroms, only to figure out in the end we are really just running into ourselves over and over again.

If we can't prove books, fossils, the light arriving from distant stars, and our memories weren't formed a few ticks before this utterance, then what *can* we prove?

And where does proof's lack leave us?

With such a question coiled inside you, how do you kick off caring differently?

How do you rise from the kitchen table, the one you're sitting at as you read this, having finished your coffee that was never brewed, finished the phone call that never transpired with a sister who exists only as your brain's phantom limb?

How do you live never having been alive?

THE PNEUMATICS OF SCALE

Unless the subject-matter of that previous section, along with the one preceding it, may prove to be the contents of two separate handwritten diary entries jotted over the course of two days, perhaps four, positively no more than five, by a character in his sixties sitting in the kitchen of some shadow-filled sixth-floor walkup housed in a cell phone video game whose theme is loneliness and puzzlement, played by a twenty-two-year-old German foreign-exchange student in her grubby room somewhere in Yangon, weakly aware of last night's chicken curry hanging in the muggy motionless air.

TRAVEL AS A SATURDAY AFTERNOON

Just like that, the inside of Ed's head became a hall of mirrors. Nothing was obvious. Everything was crooked, multiplied. He needed a nap. That's what he needed. It didn't matter what time it was. It didn't matter it was only—

What time was it, anyway?

He checked his phone. It was already four in the afternoon. Except it had been nine in the morning a few thoughts ago.

Had he really been sitting at the kitchen table all day?

Ed rubbed his forehead, flustered and slow.

When he lowered his hand and looked out the window to see if the wall was still there, he noticed it was raining. Only it wasn't raining rain. It was raining something else.

Blood streams intertwined down the windowpane.

Soon he couldn't make out the brick wall.

The kitchen glowed a soft muffled red.

I, Ed said. *I, I, I.*

Trying to convince himself.

A FRIDAY DAYBREAK

Eduard was no longer seventy-eight or eighty-seven or whatever it wasn't.

He was the sleepy little boy sitting next to his parents and sister in a honeydew-green aluminum lawn chair on the rooftop of that motel in St. George, Utah.

The atrocious desert.

The striated cinnabar formations, geometric, harsh, hovering in the cornflower dawn.

Later today, in another life, his father will fall for a college girl at the grocery store on East Tabernacle Street so crazy bad he will come to beat her regularly merely to keep feeling that electric charge he first felt a little longer.

His father sat beside Eduard, counting down from ten as if counting down to his family's unmaking.

At zero, a bluewhite flash hurtled toward them from fifty miles away, a tidal wave of resplendence, and next they were drowning in light, heat, mouths stretched open in shock, molecular structures flying apart, the atoms comprising them scattering into glitter and ash and piercing whine.

A THURSDAY NOCTURNE

Edda buoys at bedtime far out in a sea the color of precipitous worry.

Blueberry blue.

No, darker.

Plum.

Violet.

Eggplant purple.

A WEDNESDAY SOONER OR LATER

Eádweard awoke rummaging through his kitchen cabinets and drawers, trying to recall why he might be doing what he was doing.

All he knew was that the movements his body was making were both alarming and merry, as if he were a teenager doing something forbidden and delicious on a weekend night. When he couldn't find what he was looking for, he moved down the hall to the bedroom. Whatever it was wasn't in his dresser. It wouldn't be beneath his pillows, either. About this he was confident. The closet held promise. So he slid back the accordion doors and commenced sorting through raincoat, parka, peacoat, button-down shirts and chinos from somebody else's life.

Behind all of it stood a little girl in a sailor suit.

Where her face should have been, there was only flesh with a small lump sans nostrils for a nose and a squirming area of agitated skin for a mouth.

The girl was bald.

She lacked ears. Eádweard wasn't clear why he assumed she was a girl.

When she became aware of his presence, she turned away, scrambling without a sound for a corner in which to hide. Eádweard couldn't tell the difference between the back of her head and the front. Her shoulder sockets unhinged and relocated. It seemed she was facing him and trying to hide simultaneously.

Poor thing, poor thing, Eádweard said, letting his clothes fall back into place. I've fed you long enough.

He closed the accordion doors and walked out of the room.

So, he said, moving up the hallway, *that's* where I left my future.

A TUESDAY AT 3:00 A.M.

At the outset of each night during his sophomore year at NYU, Eddy slept well. Within the first half hour, though, his massive roommate breached into snores across the face-to-face desks and faux-brick linoleum flooring separating their beds. That's when Eddy started to fuss, moving through a succession of feasible sleep positions in order to settle back into his favorite opalescent emptiness, yet growing increasingly adrenalized by his roommate's wheezes and snorts.

Sooner or later Eddy surrendered, reached over, picked up his phone from his nightstand, and began playing *Remote*.

Remote was a game that wasn't a game. A little black square representing Eddy approached little congregations of other little black squares representing potential friends. The other little black squares puffed away from the Eddy square just fast enough so it couldn't possibly catch up. Sometimes the congregations consisted of three or four squares, sometimes ten or twelve. It didn't matter how many there were, or how hard Eddy tried to run after them. They outpaced him every time, leaving him floating alone until another congregation appeared.

If Eddy played long enough, the screen started silvering out, which made him feel as if he were wafting among cloudbanks.

Eventually the screen faded to black and Eddy couldn't locate himself anywhere and the game that wasn't a game was over and he knew the application wouldn't allow him to play and fail to connect with other simulated human beings again for another eighteen hours.

A MONDAY EVENTIDE

Eddie was Ruthie and Ruthie was Eddie and nothing was distinct anymore and there they were coming to awareness among the sweetness of leaves and mulch. The atrocity in their lower torso, they understood instantly, would be their life now. It would be their shattering always. They rotated their head and vomited, reached up to determine if their face were still intact, wiped away the blood puddled in their eye sockets. They wondered if their organs were still inside them or outside, if they were still one being or if the crash had torn them into many. Twenty feet beyond the pain they could make out an exquisite illumination: headlights through a haze of fine dust, the shiny green convertible Oldsmobile 88 resting on its side in the night, windshield smashed, passenger door swung wide. That's when time commenced coming back to them in the form of a voice, rhythms measured, tone habitual—a doctor's—yes—some skinny guy in his thirties with thinning linen-colored hair, forehead a field of whiteheads. He was speaking to them from the recliner beside their hospital bed, his light blue shirt two sizes too big for him, explaining how their world would be different hereafter, how things being the way things are meant they would never stay the same—because Jackson's flight, the months ahead getting used to the wheelchair, the reconfigurations, recalibrations, and yet, the doctor added (as if this were the wisdom claim, the piece of what he had to offer that would make all the other pieces fall into place and set in motion some inexplicable sense of consolation), people go through these challenges every day and somehow track down a way to reckon, adjust, accommodate, fight, and ultimately come to manage, dig up some belief to get through the years remaining to them—at which point they looked up at him, stared his horseshit down, and said: *What the fuck do I care about other people? This is mine, the same way the road next to a speeding car rips backward and you can't do anything about it. Don't talk like you have something to say just because your mouth won't stop moving*—they telling him this even as they already heard the tape in their head rewinding and playing afresh from the start, working out as they listened that this will be their soundtrack from here on out: the idiot advice, the supercilious charity, the mechanical sympathy mixed with congenital revulsion at one of the species wounded and dropping away from the herd—because poems and preachers allege we are all somehow the same deep down inside, only they are agonizingly wrong: that's the lie they like to sell us to gather acolytes and make our erect posture, bipedal motion, bulbous frontal lobes, and specialized tool use feel better about themselves, when all people really mean is *better you than me*, the human body only able to take in and store so much hurt and rage, the kind that will overflow into any room Ruthie and Eddie and Eddie and Ruthie enter like a miniature electrical storm, and it will be terrible, and it will be them, and life is so beautiful until you are forced to live it, and there is nobody to accuse and nobody to forgive and nothing to look forward to and no day on which suicide doesn't make a convincing case for itself and it will be this followed by this followed by this until that soundtrack snaps off for good.

A SUNDAY MORNING

In her mid-eighties Edie Metzger met Milo Efron at a coffee klatch hosted by one of the women from the temple to discuss current events. There was talk of wars, famines, the dying children, the collapsed buildings, the undone adults, the displaced rolling suitcases through rubbled city streets, the countless unfathomables—plus cinnamon coffee cake, a light roast of which the hostess was especially fond, and a long-retired professor with close-cropped white beard and gold wire-rimmed glasses to raise palatable ethical issues and edge the conversation away from the awkward borders of impromptu therapy sessions.

The idea was to allow the participants to exit the hostess's cozy home twice a month feeling well-informed and softly cultivated as they squalled toward their nineties.

After the discussion came an hour's socializing, the reason behind the reason everyone attended. Milo approached Edie at the kitchen island as she was easing a bite of coffee cake into her mouth, palm cupped beneath fork. He struck Edie as a brick-shaped object in a roomy gray suit with white stubble complicating his face and head. Milo wore a bright red bowtie and was arranged to ask interesting questions. Edie wore an ivory cardigan over flowery blouse and waist-defining, wide-legged ivory pants and was arranged to answer them. Doing so made her feel special, like she was being called upon by her high school teacher, one of the few who got how sharp Edie really was.

Late the next morning Milo phoned (he had taken the liberty to ask the hostess for Edie's number) and invited her out on a date to a Mozart concert at a church down the block.

Mozart left Edie cold. His music sounded like an overstuffed turkey looks on the Thanksgiving table. All those notes spilling out onto the serving platter were sure to cause heartburn. Edie was also fairly sure she had read somewhere Mozart suffered both from Tourette's and an obsession with clocks. Deep down where her morals went about their business, she could approve of neither.

She said yes on the spot.

It wasn't that she especially liked Milo. She didn't. She found him—how to say it? She found him common, if she were being completely honest with herself. Edie put it this way: He had the personality of a stray thought.

Sitting beside him at the concert, she couldn't concentrate on the piano concerto.

When she closed her eyes, she saw a vast pile of books burning at night in the middle of a square, sensed a love that had fled from her years ago, pictured the irresistible blue eyes she had met once upon a time and lived inside for a few months, yet now couldn't help recollecting forever.

At the end of that date, Milo asked her on another.

Edie said she was unfortunately busy because that's what her mother, divorced and aggrieved through the last two-thirds of her days, had taught her to say to men inviting her out on dates. So Edie went home and wandered her apartment, waiting for his next call with a clenched tummy and an insomniac's awareness of how time every so often comes to resemble a dust devil rather than minutes or days.

She carried her phone in the pocket of her peach waffle robe, promising herself she wouldn't pick up if his number appeared on her screen, even as she periodically checked to confirm she hadn't inadvertently missed his call.

It took Milo a week to try again.

Edie had her phone out and up to her ear before she knew what her hand and arm had prearranged behind her back.

For forty years before retiring, Milo had been an accountant. He was methodical and Republican, gentle and flat. He listened carefully to what Edie had to say, recalled it in detail, and was a thoughtful man, which meant he was by no means the best, by no means the worst—one of those boyfriends Edie knew she wouldn't think about that often once she had left him, but, when she did, it would be with an ill-defined affection.

Milo was a human holding pattern. For a while, he would provide pleasant company, another human voice to animate the stillness that Edie's life had become. Even though she didn't like the way he slurped the matza ball soup she had made for him, she could sense how much he wanted to step into tomorrow with her. Even though he licked his fingers as if eating invisible fried chicken while calculating her taxes at the kitchen table, he always opened doors for her and told Edie how much he enjoyed her companionship.

That made her feel sorry for him, which made her care for him more, which made her care for him less, although she couldn't quite put any of it into words.

THE LIMBIC SYSTEM

Besides, there were all those recollections from before spinning through Edie's amygdala, hippocampus, and cerebellum.

She didn't want any of them to flitter out, because snuggled inside was where she felt most herself, alert, injured, tipsy—even as she understood that wallowing in the past led exactly ... where?

Wallowing in the past led to exactly the same address that wallowing in the present or future did.

Who cares?

Those recollections were hers.

Who cares?

Those recollections were her.

ZONE OF AVOIDANCE

Edie at last agreed to move in with Milo.

More or less.

She kept her own apartment to convince herself she was her own person, nothing permanent, and at this stage of one's life the concept of *relationship* took on the qualities of a unique and complex mirage. For several days each week she lived with Milo in his larger, nicer refurbished apartment in Prospect Heights. For several she escaped back to her own to rediscover the stillness and solitude she realized she enjoyed more than she had once been capable of admitting to herself.

When she was with Milo, she wanted to be alone. When she was without him, she wanted to be cuddled against him. When she was cuddled against him, her fear diminished and her impatience grew.

GEOGRAPHY OF MONOSYLLABLES

Over time, they founded a shared country whose contours altered hourly. Often miles of woodland or opinions separated them, and sometimes Milo's fat white cat Chumsa, who did very little except sleep, eat, and judge. It wasn't unusual for the spaces Milo and Edie occupied to be shot through with a tense muteness because of something he had said offhandedly, or not said, or done, or forgotten to do, and which she could seldom call precisely or completely to mind after the fact—not that that prevented her from falling deep into herself and replying to him in monosyllables through whole afternoons and evenings.

OCCUPYING LACUNAE

One Tuesday it caught Edie as she was easing down onto her knees to plug in the vacuum behind Milo's sofa, black leather with stainless steel legs (if she didn't take the initiative, his apartment would stay bachelor-frowzy forever): she resented him for reminding her constantly of who she was.

THIS QUEEN OF NIGHTMARES

Then there were what Edie came to think of as The Great Unfastenings. Beneath each letter in the bloated leatherbound address book she bought when she was thirty-two, for instance, there were now more names crossed out than present. She had carried a headful of dense black hair well into her late seventies, only to have palm-sized spiders of it commence turning up in the bathroom sink as she crossed into her eighties, sticking to the shower tiles, defying her stylist to invent a cut to hide Edie's forfeitures. What hair remained faded to a mousy gray. She was all of a sudden cold all the time. She stopped sweating and had to eat twice as much to stay the same weight even though she had zero appetite.

And then yesterday happened: waiting for an elevator at the King's Plaza Shopping Center, Edie's bowels let go without warning.

She was standing there by herself, daydreaming, on the hunt for new bedding that she couldn't have cared less about. In the midst of imagining in the grammar of floral patterns, she became attentive to a quick loosening in her gut. Before she could react, the stink of death welled up around her, her waist-defining, wide-legged ivory pants stuffed with her own deterioration, hot portions of herself sliding down the backs of her legs.

That's how she had to maneuver to the restroom to rinse off what she could. Several alarmed younger women tried to help her, which only made Edie angry. She told them to mind their own business.

That's how she had to bus up Utica Avenue and Kings Highway to walk home from the Blake Avenue stop.

That's how she had to remember herself from now on.

Furious at her organs, Edie barged into her apartment, down the hall, straight into the shower. She made the water hot as she could take and undressed in its attack of steam and spray. For the next forty minutes she lathered and scrubbed, her waterlogged clothes clotted in the corner, recalling how telling and retelling stories keeps us alive and keeps us dead at the same time.

At long last she stepped out, toweled off, dressed in her peach waffle robe, and headed into the kitchen to make herself a cup of coffee and call Milo—not to tell him what her body had pulled on her, but simply to hear his voice in her heart.

That's when she came across his note magneted to the fridge: *I'm not interested in a superficial, non-relationship relationship. I wish I were but I'm not. Goodbye. Thank you. Goodbye. —M.*

COHERENCE IN THE TIME OF TIMELESSNESS

Dizzy, Edie read the note twice, as if she were decoding a language invented forty seconds ago, and all at once recognized how deeply in love with Milo she really was, which made her hate herself, then hate him, then call up a previous existence in which Edie had been a tiny bioluminescent fish resting on the floor of the Marianas Trench nearly seven miles beneath the surface of the ocean in heavy black hush.

For five thousand thirty-seven years, her purpose had been to hold the world together.

AIR AT SUNRISE HAS NO KNOWLEDGE

Rather than make a pot of coffee, Edie ended up pouring herself a glass of inexpensive red wine and taking a seat on her living room couch. She looked nowhere, thought nothing, poured herself a second when she was done with the first, a third when she was done with the second. Nebulous, she went to bed even though it wasn't five o'clock in the afternoon yet. The moment her head touched pillow, she tumbled into a dream about Milo in which he wanted to treat them to a day in the country. He rented a sporty green convertible Mazda MX-5 Miata and picked her up in front of her apartment building. They drove far into rural Connecticut, top down, sunshine acute, Duke Ellington on the radio. That slow piano. That honeyed alto sax. Highway dissolved into winding back roads flanked by woods strewn with mossy boulders and fast white streams, and before long they bumped past the remnants of a stone fence and rolled to a stop in a wide grassy meadow. Milo didn't talk. Edie didn't, either. They learned they had nothing to say to each other, and that that was all right. Somehow behind their wordlessness Edie knew they had had a child together decades earlier, a little girl with a cleft lip, even though they had been unmarried and not quite in love. The girl's name was—Edie couldn't remember what the girl's name was. That was all right, too. Milo and she had come to the conclusion at the time that they were too young to be parents. He admitted he couldn't bring himself to care about a baby, not then, probably not ever, and she admitted she couldn't bring herself to raise a little girl on her own. Edie thought of herself as a mother the same way she thought of herself as a green gorilla. So they put the little girl up for adoption and right away knew they had miscalculated. That's when they began making an art out of forgetting while being unable to forget, disliking each other while pretending otherwise. Sitting next to Milo, Edie grasped between one breath and the next that it was time to get out of the car and walk away from her life. Everything had become everything, and everything was too much. At heart, she came to understand, she was a fugitive. There was no more to put into this world. So she swung open her door. Milo didn't even turn to say goodbye. He continued facing forward, taken with the first burnt oranges whisking across the paling sky, how that color turned the trees into a wide black webwork. Edie strolled past the stone fence and down the dirt road, onto a paved one, and, as the evening cold began to set in, came across an inn, white with black shutters, where she took a room, having unexpectedly found her purse slung over her shoulder. When did she remember to bring it along? Her credit card was inside—her credit card, a bent paperclip, a single stick of Wrigley's spearmint gum, and nothing else. She slept in her clothes and woke realizing she would never be able to leave Milo, not in any meaningful way. Their bodies might gain distance from each other, but the rest of them would always remain interwoven. Many stories had been and would stay part of her, only not the one about leaving him. So she walked back to the remnants of the stone fence and entered the wide grassy meadow. The Miata sat in the middle of a freezing cornflower dawn, the grass and mud around it frosted and hard. Nearing, arms clutched across her chest for warmth, Edie could make out Milo sitting behind the steering wheel, exactly as she had left him, apparently still staring up at the sky through the webwork tree line—except that wasn't it. Coming even with the driver's side, Edie saw Milo was enveloped in a chrysalis of ice perhaps half an inch thick. His head was tilted far enough back that, when Edie followed his line of sight, she could tell he must have been stargazing all the way into his death. His eyes were open wide beneath the glaze, his skin gently lilac. Sometime during the night, his mouth had formed into a small italicized *o* of wonder.

ELLIPSIS AS THE PERFECTION OF THOUGHT

Edie winced into brain storm. She could hear the noisy darkness all around her, taste mold spores in muggy air. She opened her eyes, glanced down, inspected through rice-paper flesh the glowing cherry heart pumping inside her ribcage like those of some translucent fish that lives in caves.

She was—where was she?

In her bed.

That's right.

She had been sleeping. Hadn't she? Only now she had to get out. That's all the knowledge she owned. She had to get out this second. Edie had no idea what she was supposed to do after that, but she couldn't stay here.

So she threw back the sheets and tried to stand. She sat down. Her legs weren't working. She patted blackness, located her walker's frame, eased into an osteoporotic stoop, wobbled, waiting unsteadily for her balance to consolidate.

Edie had heard something.

She was sure she had heard something.

That's what had woken her: it was—what was it?—it was a woman's scream in the corridor.

It was something brutal.

She couldn't locate the door to her room. She pawed through obscurity, bleary, and ended up inside her closet, swatting old clothes away from her face.

Recalculating, she shuffled down the hall.

In the living room, exasperated, she discovered she couldn't locate her front door either. It must have shifted a few feet to the left since she last checked. Which was when? Yesterday? And when she did finally find it, the doorknob was higher than she remembered. The lock and bolts lower. The light switch next to it was gone altogether.

Edie sorted things out deliberately, thoroughly, working down an invisible flowchart, gave herself a few seconds, opened the door (which seemed much wider than usual), and shuffled into dark.

There must have been another power outage.

Hello? she said.

Nobody answered.

Everyone was still sleeping.

But the young woman—where was the young woman?

Edie pushed forward three steps in her walker, became uncomfortable with what was happening, the tiny idea flicking on in her brain that what had occurred to that young woman could occur to her if she weren't careful.

So she resolved to return to her apartment, phone the police, let them know what she had heard, and go back to sleep.

She was immensely tired.

Things would feel different in the morning.

Everything would untangle once she had had a replenishing set of—

Only try as she might she could no longer track down her door. All her right hand touched was wall—and not the painted drywall she anticipated. Instead, she found herself in what seemed to be some sort of long narrow passage, roofless, sides grainy cement.

Pausing, glancing up, Edie believed maybe what she was seeing above her were a few stars.

How could that be?

Where—

Hello? she said again.

She halted, leaning on her walker for support, arms trembly, waiting for a reply, weighing the pros and cons of making her location known. After all, if it had been a woman's scream, if whatever had caused it might still—

All she had to do was find her door.

Hello? she said a little louder, surprising herself. Can someone help me?

Maybe it wasn't a woman's scream after all. Maybe it was something else. For that matter, maybe it was her own scream. Maybe Edie had screamed herself awake, trying to outrun some horror. Maybe that's what it was.

She couldn't recall anything with specificity, but she had the dim impression something like that had gone on many times before and she was just now recollecting it.

In any case, she was sure of one thing: she was sure she wanted to get back into her apartment and get back into her bed. A few more hours' sleep and she'd be fine. Lately she couldn't get through the night and couldn't stay alert through the day. Everything felt like time slur between violent naps.

She needed to find her apartment and go back to bed. Afterward, she could brew herself a nice pot of coffee, scroll through the headlines at her kitchen table, and start her day all over again.

Sometimes that's all you could do—start your day over again until it got itself right.

Edie moved in the opposite direction down the passage, now and then stopping, stretching out her fingers like a blind person to search for her door. But it was grainy cement wall or black air mixed with her growing apprehension. Every once in a while she gathered herself and said, loud as she could manage (for some reason she couldn't raise her voice above a polite, conversational tone): Hello? This is Edie Metzger. I'm in 6B. If you can hear me, I need some help. I seem to be lost.

All the deficits inside her made her woozy.

At one point she thought about sitting down where she was, yet she also knew if she did she wouldn't be able to get up again. Her legs weren't well today. It felt as though her bones were unhurriedly disintegrating beneath her flesh.

Edie was impressed by how inhuman the human body was.

At the end of the narrow passage, she stepped out into a—what was this place?—some kind of old overgrown courtyard.

No, that can't be right.

That can't be right at all.

How could she have made her way outside?

Edie was sure there wasn't a rooftop terrace she had somehow failed to learn about all these years.

And yet there she was. Large wet ferns surrounded her in ashen light, huge misshapen trees, and, beneath one, a broken-backed park bench. Perhaps she could take it easy there for a while, get her bearings, think things through.

She took a step forward.

Her walker sank into loam an inch or two.

To make any progress whatsoever, she had to jerk the contraption out of the loam, let it drop a little way ahead, then pull herself forward to catch up. The work was draining. The muscles in her arms seared.

She advanced slowly, after a long while reaching where she thought the bench should have been, only to discover it wasn't there. Edie raised her head and took in her surroundings. She could no longer see where she had come from because fronds and giant tree trunks blocked her view.

Her lungs strained in the sogginess. She really did need to sit down somewhere. Give her a few minutes, and she was sure she could root out a way back to her apartment. In the morning she could go about her day as if none of this had taken place. All she had to do was—

What did she have to do?

The ashen light had already begun dimming out around her. Soon it would be difficult to distinguish anything at all. Except—except wasn't it supposed to be the other way around? Wasn't night supposed to be melting into dawn?

This place isn't meant for people like me, thought Edie.

Perhaps she could lean against one of those giant trunks. At least that way she could take some weight off her lower back, which had begun to throb. When she maneuvered up to one, reached out and touched the thing with her palm, its surface was awful—slick, sticky, like something's skin. She couldn't stand the notion of leaning her whole body against it, so she tottered in place a little longer, elbows and shoulders burning, back aching, then gave up and pressed forward as the last light faded out around her.

Did that mean she had somehow already spent a whole day here?

Slick fronds brushed against her face. They made her cheeks and lips prickle and go numb. Edie contemplated giving up and lying down where she was and simply—what? Simply waiting.

Surely someone would stumble across her in due course and help her back to her apartment—though, now that she thought about it, she was having some trouble recollecting the precise number.

She had known it seconds ago.

Obviously she had.

It's where she had lived for decades.

Don't lose your wits, she told herself. Just give it some time. It will come back to you when you need it.

No doubt it was on the sixth floor, right next to the stairwell.

No doubt it was the third door on the left.

If she thought about it too hard, Edie knew, she would frighten herself into losing track of it entirely. The same was true with her phone number, which it struck her she hadn't used in so long it wasn't where she had left it in her head anymore.

She was reminded of those tests the doctors gave you, the ones where they listed six objects, changed the subject, talked about this and that for a time, and then, as if you weren't expecting it, asked you to name those objects in order. She couldn't stand their fake benevolence when you got flustered and couldn't recall them, though you always understood there would be a penny and an apple in the list somewhere.

Edie decided she didn't approve of this universe at all.

When she made it back into her bed, she had every intention of sleeping the day away. It was clear that sleeping was all this day was good for. Sometimes it was like that. Some days she couldn't even recall having lived. They were the ones that made it seem as if the calendar had snapped ahead when she wasn't paying attention. It was Monday. It was Saturday. It was March. It was September. At her age, what were a few hours or months more or less?

It was stupid to keep counting as if they would add up to something.

Edie felt better pretending all time existed all at once, that it wasn't really a relentless arrow piercing her optimism a bit more every minute.

On the cusp of lowering herself onto the loam, she reached out her left hand for balance and encountered grainy cement. She was back at the wall. How did that happen?

Should she go right?

Left?

She closed her eyes and listened.

If she were outside, she should be able to hear street sounds and aim for them.

Only she couldn't hear a thing.

Her lungs hurt.

Her throat was very dry.

What in the world is wrong with me? she said out loud.

It seemed to her she were pronouncing the words phonetically.

She lifted her walker and set it down a foot in front of her and—

And next Edie had taken a tumble.

Her legs had had enough and given way beneath her.

All at once she was lying on her side, ribs pounding, right wrist smarting, flummoxed at the swift absence of verticality.

She wondered: did she just fall, or had she been lying like this for a long time?
She had no way of telling.
What she could tell was that she had to get up.
Edie had to get up right now or she would never be able to navigate her way out of this place.

She therefore lay there, gathering strength, condensing it into what she imagined as a bright ball of light in the middle of her being. Gradually she eased up onto her elbows, her knees, started waving her hand in front of her tentatively, crawling in wider and wider circles, until she bumped into her walker. It had toppled onto its side. She righted it and used it as a ladder to wrestle herself up over the twang in her joints.

Erect, shaken, aching, spent, she started out once more.
Her right wrist burned.
Her jaw hammered.
She told herself: *Just three steps. Good. Okay, Edie. Now just three steps more.*

It wasn't long before she was back at the wall, following it to the right. Her full body weight must have come down on her wrist. She worried she may have fractured it. Each pulse looked like blue summer lightning shimmering across her synapses. And her jaw: it must have hit something hard on the way down. A tree limb. A rock. She palpated the swelling. A tooth may have come loose. Now she would have to deal with setting up doctor and dentist appointments as well as everything else.

Would this day never leave her alone?

It seemed to be reaching around from behind her as she tried to ignore it and delivering little slaps.

Once comfy in her own apartment, slept out, she would have to think about all this. Now, though, the only thing she wanted was to think about was where her damn door was. She had left it open. She remembered that much. It should be easy enough to pinpoint if only she could—

And then Edie was plummeting.

While she was gone, her building must have rearranged itself again.

Edie Metzger was falling through black.

She didn't experience what came next.

She didn't experience what she experienced.

She didn't see the brawny man falling beside her, hands at his throat, wheezing, struggling for breath.

She didn't think: *If I have to go away, may it be among the thunder and lightning of one of Jackson's canvases.*

She couldn't make out the ground bolting up to meet her.

This feeling of growing smaller and smaller.

This feeling of love streaming in the wrong direction.

The unthoughts of a white cat passing through her like wind.

Everybody she had known strobing, only
in the past.

She wishes she were singing.

She was sorry she had lived.

Sorry she hadn't.

This red ocean pouring in.

This brusque disconnection from her life.

This terse conversion into

For seven seconds, Edie Metzger felt as if she were living inside a miracle. She felt as if she were flying, everything lasting a thousand years.

And then it didn't.

THE ENCYCLOPEDIC FLAYING GAME

Listen: nobody is born It. Within minutes that changes. There is no way around this fact. The players are sometimes referred to as The Hidings-and-Seekings, sometimes as The It-Looks-Like-Wars or The Belief-Skinned-Beasts. The goal of this game is to run for your life. Learn to sprint. Learn to dodge and roll. Duck. Jump. Pretend to be a stone. A bright orange poppy along the side of the highway. Become the hunted. Become the knife. Become the first-aid kit or the parachute. Drive your car into a lake. Ride a bus to the end of the line, unable to solve the schedule. Make up new rules as you go along. Don't make up new rules as you go along. Eventually you will find yourself standing alone in your stuffy bedroom with a clothes hanger in one hand and your past in the other. Reach up just below your chin. When the time is right, you will detect a zipper. Pull. Due to years of disuse, you may need to marshal WD-40, mineral spirits, resolve, exert unexpected force. Soon, however, your skin will have become a second entity draped beside you. Fold it carefully over the hanger as you would a suit. Place the occupied hanger on the clothes stand that has just appeared in the corner. That one. Yes. What a surprise. Now sit on your bed, blood seeping from your muscles, staining your white sheets pink, and say these words: *Every building appears sacred when burning.* If you are a woman, two girls will enter. If a man, two boys. They will both be you and holding hands, one carrying a black velvet bag, one a pair of pliers. The latter will be employed gently to fish among your refuse and extract each organ with love and mercy, the former to sack what once helped you palpate and judge. The penultimate to go will always be your tongue, the last always your eyes. You do not need to thank your deliverers. You do not need to damn them. They have known what you would say if you could, what you would see if you could, from the day you entered the world. Rather, brace yourself. Calm yourself. Take deep breaths. Relish the disarticulation of your argument. When this round concludes, everyone will change names and a new one begin.

ACKNOWLEDGMENTS

ENORMOUS THANKS to The Rockefeller Foundation Bellagio Center, at which I began this novel while finishing another; Michelle Dotter for her meticulous editorial eye, endless energy, and enduring support; and *Socrates on the Beach* and *Conjunctions*, in which the first and second movements of *Absolute Away* appeared, respectively, in slightly different form, as well as *Big Other* and *Café Irreal*, in which snippets of the third movement were published.

ABOUT THE PRESS

DZANC BOOKS is an award-winning independent press and a 501(c)3 nonprofit organization, created to advance unique idiosyncratic writing, to champion writers who don't fit neatly into the marketing niches of for-profit presses, and to publish debut and established authors of literary merit. In an industry increasingly driven by profits and a narrow field of bestsellers, Dzanc strives to remain a bastion of deep-thinking, original work and community outreach through our Writer-in-Residence programs, low-cost mentorship programs, and our robust internship program.

Dzanc's publishing initiatives and community programs are made possible through the invaluable support of state and federal grants and donations from corporations, foundations, and our dedicated community of readers and supporters who believe in the transformative power of the written word. Dzanc receives operational support from the national Endowment for the Arts (NEA), the Michigan Arts & Culture Council (MACC), ArtWorks.gov, and other benefactors.